summer burns

summer burns

a novel by mary jo pollak

INSOMNIAC PRESS

Edited by Lynn Crosbie.
Copy edited by Peter Darbyshire.
Designed by Mike O'Connor.

Canadian Cataloguing in Publication Data

Pollak, Mary Jo, 1958-
    Summer burns

ISBN 1-895837-49-9

I. Title.

PS8581.O315S94 1999   C813'.54   C99-931680-X
PR9199.3.P559S94 1999

The publisher gratefully acknowledges the support of the Canada Council and the Ontario Arts Council.

Printed and bound in Canada

Insomniac Press, 393 Shaw Street,
Toronto, Ontario, Canada, M6J 2X4
www.insomniacpress.com

POLL

With deep gratitude to Lynn Crosbie and Michael Holmes for their encouragement and help, and much thanks to family and friends for their support — especially my husband, Steve

To Ann and Donna

part 1
first summer

the planets

"Want to go to the Purple Palace?"

Hesitation. Just to make it look convincing. "Um… Okay." Waiting forever for Sandy to ask. Everyone there is friendly to her, but somehow Joan does not feel comfortable showing up on her own. Sandy is her passport. Because Sandy made it her business to have the inside edge on everything that went on in town.

Kind of a miserable day, but there had been some spring teasers, so Joan and Sandy are optimistic about good times to come. May 24th weekend coming up, school out soon. Joan is already wearing the new spring jacket she bought in Toronto. Could not wait to show it off. But now she is cold. It is kind of misty with a few drops of rain falling. Smattering of new green buds standing out brightly against the drabness of the day. It is a long walk to the Palace. Beyond the year-round homes, down the hill to the beach, along a meandering gravel road lined with boarded-up cottages.

Joan is excited. Even though she does not really like Uranus. And does not have a chance with Mars as far as she can see. Just to be able to casually mention that she had been at the Purple Palace. These guys are like legends. Heroes. Close to rock stars. They certainly know everything about rock stars and music. They always have the latest albums and rock magazines.

Two guys who never left at the end of last summer. Nobody

remembers where they are from. Windsor? London? Stuck around all winter in the little mauve cottage, just barely winterized enough to make it livable. The rent is dirt cheap off-season. Neither of them work. Someone is always there and they can get you whatever you want. And they are not bikers. Usually everything dries up during the winter but not this year. Plus there is a guaranteed party at their place nearly every weekend. If you have an in.

Everybody has forgotten their real names since the nicknames took hold. Mars and Uranus. Mars, because he is kind of spacey and cool. Guys in town do not stand a chance against him. Girls all holding their breath to see who manages to get him. He does not really get involved with anybody. A couple of girls claim to have fucked him, but nobody is sure if they are really telling the truth. The ones who boast of it do not seem to come around to the Purple Palace much afterwards. Keeps a lot of breathing space around him. He is distant with guys, too. Except Uranus.

Uranus, because he is an asshole. Good looking, Joan supposed. Somehow a twisted version of Mars. An added roughness to his features. A skewing of lines that makes him not quite handsome. Still, a lot of girls go for him. He flirts a lot with everybody. Almost everybody. Not with Joan, which suits her fine. Sandy and Uranus have a love-hate relationship. He has fucked practically everybody in town except Joan and Sandy. Or it seems like that.

The guys are home. B.J. Tremblay is there, too. Big John. Also a very interesting guy. Not really a local. His family moved to town some years ago. Outsiders who keep to themselves. Joan and Sandy can see the three guys through the big front window of the cottage. Joan smiles, thinking about her friends' faces at school on Monday. Green with envy. All the guys look up as Joan and Sandy get to the door. Something is grabbed off the coffee table. Joan often thinks the guys see them as drug sponges. Probably true about Sandy.

Uranus is smiling at Sandy when he opens the door, though. Joan hangs back, waiting. Uranus steps outside the door. "What do you want, bitch?" But friendly.

"Nothing from you."

"Good, because we were just going out." Uranus starts to retreat back into the cottage.

Joan's heart skips, but Sandy moves forward, wedging herself in the open door. "Come on, we walked all this way. Where are you going anyway?"

Uranus kind of gives way. Turns to check Mars's face. Sandy pushes past. She is all the way into the cottage. Joan shuffles on the door jamb. Keeping her back to the metal screen door. Pushing against it so that it is still a crack open. Neither Mars nor Uranus answer Sandy's question. Sandy marches over to the stereo and picks up a Genesis album.

"Hey, I saw this concert. Were you there?" Long discussion about Genesis, the concert, other bands. Sandy is now sitting down. Joan is unsure if they are really welcome. She is still standing by the door. Uranus has dropped the Genesis album onto the turntable and the music is blasting at top volume. Joan can hardly hear the conversation. When music is playing she has a hard time focusing on anything else. Often she cannot understand the talk going on even when people are right beside her because the music steals her ears. She loves Genesis. Saw the concert with Sandy. She is kind of drifting when she realizes B.J. is talking to her.

"Come in. Sit down."

Sandy and Joan sit with their jackets on. On the edges of their seats. For a long time. Joan tries to read the guys' faces to see if they really want them to be there. Wherever they are planning to go, they do not seem in a hurry. A lot of the time Mars, Uranus, and B.J. pretty much ignore Sandy and Joan. They talk about drugs that are around town lately, what might be coming in soon. There is some good stuff. Hesitation, then Uranus brings out a bag, and a joint is rolled and passed around. Yes. It is good. Now there is nothing but the music in Joan's ears.

The room is pretty hot. Electric heater blasting in one corner. The guys and Sandy are sunk back comfortably in the couch and one easy chair that furnish the cottage living room. Sandy now has her jacket off. Joan removes hers. Joan is sitting on a brightly painted wooden kitchen chair. She feels like she is going to pass out. Wishes she had the deep-cushioned, musty old chintz chair that Sandy is sprawled across. Even if it is completely filthy. Looks like used gotchees and a pair of dirty socks wadded into the corner. Is that a skid-mark on the gotchees? There is a *Hustler* spread out on the coffee table. A major beaver shot right there in front of her eyes. She cannot stop looking at it. She looks out the window. She looks around the room. But every few minutes she becomes aware that her eyes have drifted back. She looks up and sees B.J. smiling at her. She turns red.

She wants a cigarette, but her throat is dry. After a few minutes she convinces her body to get up from the chair. Now that she is standing, she feels better. Head clearing. Water would be good. Legs propel her to the kitchen. She makes it without bumping into any furniture. Or tripping over any of the guys' outstretched legs. Pretty proud of herself. Man, is she fried. Kitchen is disgusting. No clean dishes at all.

"Why don't you make some tea?" calls Sandy.

Joan thinks this is pretty presumptuous, but the guys do not seem to object. Well. Have to do the dishes. The thing is... when you are stoned...at least for Joan when she is stoned... she cannot stop cleaning once she gets started. Really, it becomes a pleasure. Especially in this kitchen, because everything is so yucky. She can really make a mark.

"You don't have to do this."

"I can't help it." Blurted out. She must sound like some sort of sick person.

It is now mid-July. School is out. Joan has a job as a waitress. Sandy is working at her mother's tourist cabins. Cleaning, taking care of guests. They are over at the Palace a lot. Every time Joan gets stoned when she is here, she cleans the kitchen. Which is pretty much every time they come. She finds it easier to slip into the kitchen. The music is not so loud in the kitchen. If anybody really wants to talk to her they can come out to the kitchen. Usually they just leave her alone. She is a bit startled that Mars has draped himself in the doorway. He takes out his cigarettes, offers one to her, lights it for her.

Barb wanders into the kitchen. Barb is a fixture at the Palace now. Farm girl. Bit of an oddball. Never finished high school. Could not get along with her parents, hated the farm. Lives on her own in an apartment above a store. Works as a waitress at the steak house where Joan works. They have gotten kind of close. Barb is pretty smart and interesting to talk to.

The reason Barb is always around is because B.J. is her old man. B.J. and another guy, Billbo, have moved into the Palace. Mars and Uranus decided to get room-mates because the rent went up for the summer. Barb and B.J. plan to take off on B.J.'s bike when the summer is over. Tour down to California or some-place warm. Joan thinks Barb is throwing her life away. But because Barb is always at the Palace now, Joan feels more com-fortable showing up without Sandy.

"God, you're anal!" says Barb.

Joan kind of shrugs her shoulders. Because she is too stoned she does not know how to answer. She cannot tell if Barb really wants a response. Is she expected to deliver a witty comeback, or should she go into a long history of her obsessive neatness?

Barb just giggles in her high-pitched, slightly irritating way. "Come and sit down."

Joan is finished cleaning so she agrees. She pours herself a tea and starts to follow Barb into the living room. As she brushes past Mars, who is still leaning on the door frame, he grabs her hand and presses something into it. She sees two little white tabs.

"White clinical," he whispers.

She looks at his face. He is serious. Cleaning kitchen has paid off, she guesses. She slips the tabs into the small watch pocket on her jeans.

For a change the stereo is not blasting in the living room. It is midafternoon and it is a sweltering day. Inside the cottage it is not too bad. The glass has been taken off all the windows and the screens are allowing a breeze in off the lake. Although it is not a beachfront cottage a strip of bright blue can be seen between the cottages across the road. Everybody has gone to the beach except Joan, who has gotten into cleaning; Mars, who stays behind lounging around; and Billbo, who is sleeping. Now Barb is back from her shift at the steak house. The three sit down together. The living room is very pleasant. It is actually pretty neat and clean. Maybe the guys are getting used to tidiness.

Joan is starting to straighten out. She and Barb get into a deep chat. Mars comes in and flops on the sofa, at the other end from Joan, but his legs are stretched out and his bare feet are touching her thigh, which is also bare because she is wearing cut-offs. She tries to act as if she does not notice. After a few minutes she crosses her legs so that his feet are not touching her anymore.

Sandy, Uranus and B.J. come back from the beach. B.J. scrunches into the easy chair, beside Barb, and gives her a kiss. Of all the guys Joan knows, B.J. is the only one who would do something like that. Joan thinks it is nice. B.J. is wearing nothing but cut-offs. He is slender but powerful-looking with long, well-formed muscles. Little wrinkles stretch across his washboard tummy. Maybe Barb is not so dumb about her life after all.

Uranus is complaining. "He hears I got new goods and wants me to have a party. Hey, man, this is a business I'm running. What makes him think I am going to give my shit away for nothing?"

"Like the Symbionese Liberation Army," says Joan. Everybody looks at her, puzzled. She turns red, but she explains, "You know, Patty Hearst. They kidnapped Patty Hearst."

"Oh, yeah," says Barb, "they made her rob banks."

"Ha, ha, ha," says Sandy. Just like that. It is the way she laughs. It is just like she speaks the words, only she says them really loud. She laughs a lot, too, so it is always easy to pinpoint where she is in a crowded room. "What's that got to do with anything?"

Joan glares at Sandy. Joan wrote her spring history essay on the SLA. She knows she told Sandy all about it. "The

Symbionese Liberation Army," she says carefully, "made Patty Hearst's father give away truckloads of food to the poor." Pause. "Like Robin Hood, you know."

Mars beams. "Oh, yeah, I remember…."

"Bunch of fucking commies," says Billbo, appearing at his bedroom door. Talks with his mouth full. Sweet Marie bar. He washes it down with a swig of Coke. That is practically all he eats or drinks. Morning, noon, or night. Sometimes pizza. He is a pale, scrawny guy. Does pharmaceuticals mostly. Has lots to sell even when there is nothing else around. From down in the States. He is older, over twenty-five for sure. His room at the Palace is piled with books and magazines about Hitler. On the back of his jean jacket he has a crude swastika that he drew on with a marker.

"Yeah, well I'm talking about you!" Uranus half screams at Billbo.

"You know, they don't want to hear your miss-smarty-pants stuff," Sandy tells Joan. Later. On the way home.

"Huh?"

Voice full of ridicule. "Like the Si-am-bone-ese Liberation Army," mocks Sandy. "Just because you wrote that essay…."

"Well, it just made me think of it."

"You know guys don't like girls who are too smart."

Joan knows. She has to remember to keep her mouth shut. It just popped out. Things like that were always popping out.

Up late. Almost lunch. Worked until about two last night. Some drunks that would not leave. Then she had to clean up. They did not even tip. Assholes. She is determined to enjoy her day off. This is going to be good. Pours some orange juice. Downs one of the little white tabs. By early afternoon she is tripping. Good, clean stone. Smiling. Day tripping is best. Once she was caught still flying way into the night after everybody else had crashed. Nowhere to go, nothing to do. Kind of like being in hell.

She heads down to the beach. Sandy is there with Uranus, B.J., and Billbo. One of the boys. That's Sandy. It makes her untouchable. It lets her go wherever she wants to go. That is why it is good to stick with Sandy. Joan spreads out her towel and sits with them. It is the best day so far this summer and the beach is paradise. Joan stares across the flat, clear water. Everything is absolutely perfect. Nearby somebody has a radio. Every song played is blissfully beautiful. The sun is warm on her skin. A light breeze plays with her hair. The others are laughing and joking. She feels at one with everything.

"You're tripping!"

It almost sounds like an accusation, but Joan smiles. "Uh-huh."

"What have you got?" demands Sandy.

"White clinical."

Uranus swings his head around. Looks at her intently. Looks at B.J. Looks at Billbo.

"I'm going in for a swim," says Joan.

In the water everything is perfect again. It is like looking through glass. She hangs in the fetal position underwater and watches the dappled sun patterns moving across the sand ripples on the bottom. When she drags her hands through the water distorted silver globes stream out behind them. She can stay under forever. No. She does not forget to come up for air. Acid is not like that for her. It just makes everything perfect.

When she gets out only Billbo is left sitting on the beach. A knowing smile. "What d'you do to get the acid?" She shrugs. "Mars is a really foxy guy," he says slyly. Oh. They think she screwed Mars. She thinks of the rumours that are probably spreading already.

"I'd like to fuck the asses off both of you," says Billbo. She looks at him. "Seriously. And you know what would be great? If you were both tied up."

She is still staring at him. What to say? It is kind of hard to think. The image of Mars and her. Naked. Bound together. Right now Billbo looks tiny. In the bright sun his skin is palely white. His sunglasses look gigantic on his little pinched face. He is leaning back on toothpick arms. Sunken shoemaker's chest looks like it is poked through to his spine. He looks like a weird cartoon character. She has to laugh.

He laughs, too. Then he tells her a story. He is living in the East Village in New York. A commune-type thing. Pissed off because his drugs are always being stolen. So he makes himself a stash box. It is all wired up. He puts a warning note on it. But one day he comes home and the box is gone. So he pushes the remote control detonator. Yup. He can hear the explosion. He hopes there are no innocent people hurt. He is pretty sure whoever has the box is dead.

After that Billbo gets up and leaves. Joan is wondering why he told her the story. Oh, she thinks. It was his white clinical.

The end of August. Hot and muggy. Joan has not been at the Palace for a long time. Her cheeks still burn to think about it. Mars was super pissed off. She was not supposed to tell. She was supposed to save it and do it with him. Also, she wants to stay clear of Billbo. Too scary. They are giving her more hours at the steak house anyway. Sandy keeps her filled in about everything. Even though there is a bit of a rift between Sandy and Joan after Sandy sided with Mars and Uranus. Joan and Barb are getting closer and closer. B.J. took off with a bike gang. Barb is pretty fucked up about it.

Later in the summer Mars asks Billbo to move out of the Palace. He is just getting too weird. Then Uranus gets in trouble with the cops and is gone. Rent is too high for Mars alone. Time to move on. Mars is giving one more party. A big one. This is going to be the party of the summer.

Joan, Sandy, and Barb plan to go together. They agree to meet at Sandy's because her mother will not be home. Sandy has a couple of joints she copped off Uranus before he dropped out of sight. Barb is late so Joan and Sandy share the first one together, then start to get ready for the party. Sandy has asked Joan to bring some of her clothes and she tries them on in various combinations. Joan goes through Sandy's clothes and makeup trying to find the look she wants tonight.

Barb does not show up. It is getting late. By now the party should be in full swing. They do not want to miss anything. Joan and Sandy leave. Things are really hopping when they get to the Palace. Inside they can barely move. The lawn in front is packed, too. Sandy wades into the thick of things. Joan grabs a beer and heads back outside. There is plenty happening on the lawn and it is much more pleasant there. There is room to dance on the patio. A bunch of people are really getting into it. Joan joins in. Beer. Pot. Music. She is in her own world.

"Hey, sexy mama!" Arm thrown around her neck. Joan staggers. Barb is hanging her full weight on Joan's shoulders. In one hand she holds a forty pounder of tequila with a big dent taken out of it already. She tries to force Joan to take a swig. Joan worms away. Two beers already. Does not want to get sick. She is surprised to see Uranus behind Barb. He grins.

Joan says, "I'm going to get a beer." Spins off, pushes her way into the cottage. Has to find Sandy. Lights are low and bodies press. Arms enfold her. Not Barb. These are strong, masculine arms. A face comes over her shoulder. A mouth covers her mouth. French kiss. She can hardly breathe. Struggling free. Mars! He grins at her, steps back a bit. He is naked. Nobody else has noticed yet. She stares. Confused.

"Ha, ha, ha," Sandy's laugh rises above the music. It is almost a scream. Joan remembers that she is looking for Sandy. Plunges off in the direction of the laugh. Behind her she hears a squeal. Somebody else has discovered that Mars is naked. Joan finds Sandy.

"Barb is here with Uranus." Sandy looks at her. Joan repeats.

Then Sandy is pulling her along. They get outside. No Barb. No Uranus.

"Let's find them," says Sandy. "I gotta talk to Uranus." Sandy drags Joan away from the party. Barb and Uranus have disappeared, though. Sandy and Joan end up walking all over town, but finally they give up looking. Joan looks at her watch. It is nearly four in the morning. Probably best to just go home.

Sandy phones Joan. Mars and Uranus are gone. Barb was found wandering half-clothed. Could not remember much. Alcohol poisoning. Drank the whole forty pounder. Puked until there was nothing to puke. Then puked her guts out. Sandy's voice drops to a whisper.

"Uranus. He fist-fucked her."

"What?"

"Fist-fucked. Rammed it in up to the elbow."

Joan tries to imagine. Is it physically possible? How did Sandy always find out about these things?

"Mars grabbed me and kissed me," she tells Sandy.

"When?"

"At the party. He was naked, too."

Sandy does not reply for a minute. Long pause.

"He likes you, you know."

"Huh?"

"Mars. He thinks you're smart."

Joan feels something like her heart twisting in her chest. "Why didn't you tell me?"

"I thought you knew but weren't interested."

Joan is silent. Hangs up the phone. Furious. It will take a while before she can bring herself to talk to Sandy again.

Barb kind of goes off the deep end. Turns out her dad fucked her (Sandy's inside information). That is why she left home. She acts weird. Drops out of circulation for a while. Then she disappears altogether. A couple of weeks later they hear that Uranus is killed in a crash. Nobody is really sad. By then school has started. The winter is a drag this year. There is a void left by the empty mauve cottage. Which is now blue. The owner had a lot of work to do to make it rentable again after the party. Joan keeps her job at the steak house. Works weekends and a couple of evenings a week.

Every once in a while she is gripped by a fantasy. She and Mars are tied up. Billbo has performed unspeakable deeds. Then left them. Joan is weeping. Shuddering. Hysterical. Mars consoles her. Promises revenge. Billbo will hurt. They cannot move tied face to face. It is hours before anybody finds them. By then they have both fallen asleep, Joan's cheek resting on Mars's tanned, firm chest. Mars is now helplessly in love with her. Her cheeks are red and throbbing with every heartbeat pounding in her ears.

"Hullo? Anybody in there?" She is brought back from her altered state. Sandy is sitting across from her at the waitress' table at the steak house. "So…what are you doing after work?"

"I don't know."

"Want to go down to the trails?"

"Okay."

The trails maze through the woods to the south of town. Along the shore. Past where the cottages stop. Large area of bush. Trails like arteries. If you go far enough you come out in a farmer's field. They say the trails have been there since the Indians. Every kid in town has the layout of the trails burned into their minds. Somehow by the time they grow up everybody seems to forget about them. Which makes it perfect. Young kids use them for bike trails. Older kids use them for parties when the weather is good. There are a number of spots. Clearings in the bush. Joan and Sandy are at one now.

It is spring. School will be out in a couple of weeks. After May 24th one can usually bet on a party somewhere along the trails. The spot they have chosen is pretty popular. Nobody else is there right now. Nearby, there is a little stream overhung with bushes. They find a stash of beer hidden there. They crack a couple open. It is okay. Everybody contributes when they can. Rummaging through the undergrowth for wood. Soon they have a fire going. It is getting dark. Wondering if anybody will show up. Might leave soon.

"You bitches got any papers?" Eyes wide. Joan and Sandy stare.

"You're supposed to be dead!" squeals Sandy.

"Yeah, we heard...." Joan's voice trails off. The scumbag should have died.

But Sandy is digging for papers in her bag. Hands them to Uranus, who rolls a joint. Sandy will party with anybody who has pot. Joan fumes but takes a toke. Uranus is telling his story. The guy in the crash had Uranus's wallet on him. Fit his description. Cops were looking for Uranus. Let them think he was dead. Took off down to the States. Ended up crashing at some big mansion. Non-stop party for months. Rock stars, too. Partied with David Bowie. Joan is really fuming now. How did a jerk like Uranus end up being so lucky? Uranus raving on and on about what a gas he had. Joan's attention slowly slips away. The Mars fantasy takes over again. Wonders what would have happened if she had been smart enough to read the signs. Could have been the queen of cool last summer. The one who got Mars. Maybe they would have nicknamed her Venus....

"Whatever happened to Mars?" Sandy is asking the question that Joan would have.

"Mars? Oh... Didn't I say? He was the one who died in the crash."

part 2
second summer

brandy

The guy was going a bit fast. Showing off his car. A little green MG convertible. Pretty nice, but...it is still a bit cold although it is mid-June. First weekend after school is out. Joan is riding in the back, so she does not have much protection. Up front Sandy is talking the guy's ear off. Joan cannot hear what Sandy is saying because of the wind. His eight-track is blasting at top volume, too. Every once in a while Sandy's laugh comes drifting back. "Ha, ha, ha." Joan is huddling in the back seat. Dead beer bottles shifting around her feet. At least it is sunny. The countryside whipping by is fresh and bright. Gratifying sense of freedom. Just took off hitchhiking for no reason at all.

"How about Wasaga Beach?" asked Sandy as they stood by the side of the road.

"Okay," Joan answered, actually kind of scared. Wasaga Beach is a pretty long trip. Joan is wondering if they will get back on time. Sandy does not really give a shit, but Joan usually tries not to get on the bad side of her parents. All the same, it is a huge temptation to get out on the road. Out of town. Out of Dead City. The flood of tourists will not begin until the long weekend. Not much to do in town. Joan does not even have a shift at the steak house. Could be the only Saturday of the entire summer when she does not have to work. Okay, let's go.

They get a ride almost right away. Guy whizzes by, slams on

the brakes, backs up at high speed. They both agree they like the car. Kind of dorky looking guy, though. Soft looking. Really straight haircut, except he still has not gotten rid of sideburns he probably grew because they were in a few years ago. Some kind of polyester sport shirt. Tennis shorts. Running shoes with white socks. Says he is from Guelph. That explains it.

The guy cannot take his eyes off Sandy's chest. Sandy's chest is a legend in town. Flat as a pancake until grade ten, then all of a sudden. Like within a month. Biggest boobs in the whole high school. Either Sandy does not notice or she pretends not to notice the guy ogling her breasts. She starts going on about his car. He gets a dopey proud grin. Soon he has agreed to take them all the way to Wasaga. Says he has a friend there. Joan is not too happy. She will be a Popsicle by the time they get there. Wishes she had grabbed her jacket on the way out the door.

If she was not so preoccupied with being cold she might be worried about this guy's driving. He is really moving now, and he is spending too much time looking at Sandy's boobs. Joan tries to catch Sandy's attention. Gripping her arms and rolling her eyes to show how cold she is. Sandy ignores her. Joan gets down on the floor between the seats. Piles the empties on one side of the driveshaft hump. Curls up in a ball. Head resting on the hump. It is a little warmer, but there is a constant whirlwind laden with grit and debris from the floor.

Joan asks the guy to stop so she can go to the washroom. He passes more than one gas station before he obliges her. Once they stop, Joan jerks her head at Sandy to follow her into the can. Sandy obstinately stays seated in the MG. Bitch. Joan spends several minutes warming up in front of the hand dryer in the washroom. When she comes out, the guy is at the pop machine.

"Do they have Pepsi?" yells Sandy. Surprisingly they do, although the machine has Coca-Cola emblazoned largely across the front. The guy is fiddling with change. Joan studies his squat, hairy legs. Leans toward Sandy.

"Let's ditch him here. He's a real dork."

"Uh-uh! He's going to drive us all the way."

Then the guy is back at the car. Has Pepsis for both of them. Sandy gives Joan a dirty look as if to say shut up. The guy gets in and guns the engine. Lays rubber, screeching onto the highway. Joan sips her Pepsi and tries to smoke a cigarette. Ashes and sparks fly off in the wind. Smoke in her eyes. It does not take long before Joan is ice-cold again. The guy starts talking about how dangerous it is for two attractive chicks to be hitchhiking. Going on and on about all the things that could happen to them. Now Sandy starts to pay attention to the looks Joan is sending her. The guy is starting to sound like a psycho.

They get to Wasaga Beach okay. The guy tries to get them to come to his friend's cottage. Once they are in town Joan and Sandy make some excuses and get out of the car as soon as the guy has to stop. They walk down a side road, duck between some cottages and lose him. Out of sight they both break out giggling. Helpless laughter.

"Ha, ha, ha," screams Sandy. "What a loser!"

Sandy wants to go to the beach. When they get there it is deserted. The wind is brisk and there is no shelter. Both have bathing suits on under their clothes. Always dress that way all summer. Sandy heads for the water. Calls Joan a chickenshit for not coming in with her. Joan curls up on the sand. Studies the goose pimples on her white arms and legs. Thinks she might be able to start a tan if she could bring herself to uncurl and lie flat. Then Sandy is back. She is shivering now, too, and she only waded in up to her knees.

They take a stroll up and down the strip. Wasaga is a washout. Dead, just like back in town. They poke in a head shop for a few minutes. Lots of neat stuff. All stocked up for the summer. Grim-mouthed old lady watches their every move. When they leave, Sandy opens her fist to show Joan a little stone hash pipe she copped. Nobody nervier than Sandy.

Coffee would be good. No—hot chocolate. They go into a restaurant. No way! It's Barb! Barb is there. Barb is the waitress. Big squeals from Barb and Sandy. Joan stands frozen. Just a couple of weeks ago Uranus came back from the dead. Came out of the bush and smoked a reefer with them. Now Barb reappears. Only she is telling them not to call her Barb.

"Brandy," she insists."Don't you love that song?"

Joan snorts, "Brandy and Sandy."

"Ha, ha, ha," laughs Sandy.

"It's okay," says Barb/Brandy. "We won't be hanging around."

"Why not?" asks Sandy.

"Don't tell anyone you saw me."

She got mixed up with bikers. The thing with Uranus, it was true. (Joan still cannot picture it being possible. Up to the elbow?) So, anyway, Barb/Brandy got totally freaked at first. Then depressed. Then one day B.J., her old man who took off with a bike gang, comes back. So she goes with him. Riding with the gang. At first it is okay. She is free, she is putting miles between herself and her parents. And she is with the guy she loves. Joan thinks about what Sandy told her about Barb/Brandy's father raping her. Wonders if she should let on she knows. Decides not to say anything. Barb/Brandy continues with her story. B.J. gets in trouble. He owes some other guys big. They say they will take Barb/Brandy. B.J. tries to stop them, but they beat him up badly. Barb/Brandy does not know what happened to B.J. after that.

The two guys take her with them. Down to the States. There is nothing she can do. She has no money and they say they will kill her if she tries to get away. They end up in Florida. There is a big gathering of bikers. The two guys let any of their friends use her. She thinks it will not be long before they probably kill her. So one night she gets away. The next four months she spends trying to get back to Canada without being caught. She does not know if they might come back looking for her, but she is not taking any chances.

"So you came to Wasaga, which will be crawling with bikers any day now?" wonders Joan aloud.

"Yeah, but different gangs."

Oh, thinks Joan.

Sandy starts telling Barb/Brandy about seeing Uranus. Joan tries to stop her, but Sandy just has to run off at the mouth. Barb/Brandy is super pissed off to hear what a gas he has been having after making her life so miserable. Joan is starting to get drowsy now. Warmed up by hot chocolate, melting into her chair. Her head hits the table with a clunk.

Sandy is jiggling her awake. "Here, take this. Perk you up. We've got to get going."

Joan looks at the clock nestled between two deer heads on the wall over the counter. Late in the afternoon. Yes, should leave now. So tired. She washes the red capsule down with the last of her now cold chocolate.

"Take another one. It'll probably take two."

Joan obeys. "What are they?"

"Diet pills. Got any money?"

"Why?"

"To pay for the hot chocolate?" Joan sighs. Sandy never has cash on her. Joan always pays.

They get up to go and Barb/Brandy is coming with them. Joan gives her a dazed, questioning look.

"I'm going to get Uranus."

Joan thinks, "Sandy and her big mouth." Imagines dozens of bikers coming down on them the minute they get back to town. They walk to the highway.

"I don't even know if Uranus is still around," says Joan.

This ploy does not work. "I bet he'll be back," says Barb/Brandy.

Joan glares at Sandy. Sandy seems to be relishing a confrontation between Barb/Brandy and Uranus.

They all stand with their thumbs out. It is not long before some GI Joe in an army truck stops for them. They look at each other, rolling their eyes. "Make love, not war!" barks Sandy. But they run and get in. It is a guy from town. Pimple-faced brown-noser from grade twelve. Never had a girlfriend all through high school. They stare.

"Militia," he says. Some kind of manoeuvres. He gets the truck for the night. Tomorrow he has to drive it somewhere and link up with some other guys. So he is actually heading for town. They have a ride the whole way. Joan is happy. Late afternoon sun beats in through the windshield. The cab is nice and warm.

"Hey, you used to work at the steak house?" Half question, half statement. Joan looks up. Thinks he is talking to her. But he is looking at Barb/Brandy. "Barb. Right?"

"I call myself Brandy now."

"Great name—I love that song!"

GI Joe and Barb/Brandy are hitting it off. Joan and Sandy sit quietly. They are both starting to get off on the diet pills. Joan feels a tingling in her face, especially in her lips. She settles comfortably into the seat. GI Joe is taking a shortcut along a side road. Farms and rolling hills pass by bathed in the amber sun of the late afternoon. Joan is relieved. They should be back in town by suppertime. No need to make up any excuses for her mother.

"These trucks are really powerful," GI Joe is saying. Barb/Brandy seems to be impressed. Joan groans inwardly. "Hey, watch this," he says.

He veers off the road just before a bridge and heads straight into a small river. Water parts in big waves on either side of them.

"Wow!" yells Barb/Brandy as they plow across. The truck comes grinding to a halt. GI Joe applies the gas. The engine revs. He puts it in reverse. The engine revs. He makes the girls get out into the knee-deep water. Guns the engine.

"You're hung up on a rock," Joan yells, peering under the truck.

"Ha, ha, ha," screams Sandy hysterically. She grabs Joan by the arm and pulls her away. "Come on Barb...I mean Brandy!" she yells back over her shoulder.

"I'm staying with him," says Barb/Brandy evenly. GI Joe smirks and throws his arm over her shoulder.

Joan and Sandy trudge back to the road in their squishy, wet shoes. Joan looks back to see GI Joe and Barb/Brandy locked in a kiss, his hand up her shirt. Joan and Sandy are stuck on a country back road. It is a long walk just to get to a road that might have even a little traffic on it. Dark now, and the temperature has dropped drastically. They get to a little crossroad town. Not even a town. A few houses and a gas pump. No lights on anywhere. It is like everybody in the place goes to bed when the sun goes down.

Joan is shivering and she is hungry. "Can't leave well enough alone," she mutters.

"What's that?" asks Sandy.

"You didn't have to tell Barb about Uranus. She would have been better off not knowing."

"Yeah, well…" fumbles Sandy.

"And we'd be better off, too," grumbles Joan, "not stuck out here freezing our butts off. I'm dying of hunger." Joan keeps on griping, her anger building against Sandy.

"Oh, just shut the fuck up," says Sandy impatiently. She rifles through her bag and brings out two more of the diet pills. "Here, take these and you won't be hungry anymore."

Joan hesitates, then takes the pills.

It is about 9:30 when a car finally stops. Motherly-looking middle-aged woman. Another lucky ride. Going right through to town. Joan gets in the back seat. There is a blanket there. She snuggles into it. So cold she cannot stop her lips from chattering. The woman is laying into them for hitchhiking out in the middle of nowhere late at night. Joan is not listening. She cannot really hear over her own heartbeat thumping loudly in her ears. She slips quietly into mild convulsions. Too many diet pills, she thinks. Fucking Sandy.

farm boys

Joan serves her customers with care. Better tips that way. Always has the biggest haul. Also, she likes to do her job well. When she works in the coffee shop section at the steak house she is happy to chat with the people at the counter. That is how she gets to know the guys from the Farmhouse. For once it is Joan, not Sandy, who is on the inside with the neatest guys around town that summer. Joan has the wheels to get there, too. Even though it is really her mom's car she can get it any time. Bit of a beater, but it gets them around. Big old car with wide bench seats. Can squeeze in eight, maybe even ten people.

The Farmhouse is off the beaten track. Curvy old road along the river. Every dip and turn memorized by now. Joan and Sandy have sped along it that many times. Not a wide and graded country road. Narrow, rutted, overhung with gnarled trees. An old road. Houses close to the road. Some abandoned and falling down. A pretty drive. Makes Joan's heart ache.

Three guys share the Farmhouse: Zeke the Freak, Duane (which became Duano, then Draino), and Elliot. All of them do construction work. Casual labour. They deal, too. Zeke the Freak is a reliable source. No chemicals—only pot, hash, oil. Back-to-the-earth types. Probably why they rent the Farmhouse. Besides the cheap rent. When they are working they come into the coffee shop at the steak house for lunch. Sit in their dusty clothes.

Eat with grubby hands. Zeke the Freak is the one that talks. Draino laughs at his jokes. Listening to Zeke the Freak, Joan lets her eyes stray over to Elliot. Mostly he reads while he eats.

Pretty chummy. Joan is welcome at the Farmhouse any time. A couple of times Joan goes out to the Farmhouse and finds Elliot alone. He makes her tea. Talks about the books he is reading. The last time he gave her a book by Jack Kerouac. Since then she has been hoping to catch him when the others are not around. Wants to get to know him better. Wants to tell him what she thinks about Kerouac.

Would not be doing that today. Hundreds at the Farmhouse. Zeke the Freak is holding a pig roast to raise rent money. And to have fun. Everybody is coming. Joan and Sandy are glowing with excitement. Warm, late-June day. Windows down. Booting down the road, sun flickering through the leaves. First big party of the summer.

Cannot get close to the Farmhouse. Cars parked a quarter mile in either direction. Joan has to wait for Sandy, who is picking her way along the gravel road in platform sandals. Halter top. Boobs jiggling. Jeans cut off short enough that the bottom of her ass shows. Joan is in overalls and T-shirt. Bandana. No trouble walking in her huaraches.

Big line of motorcycles parked in front of the Farmhouse. Bikers. That means the summer is really here. Joan and Sandy pick up their pace. On the other side of the Farmhouse a field stretches down to the river. There is already a big crowd. Joan sees a huge skewered pig turning on a spit. Apple in its mouth. She has never seen a whole animal being roasted before. Always thought the apple was some kind of movie cliché. They really do put an apple in the mouth. Some guy Joan and Sandy have never seen before asks them for their tickets. Five dollars if you had bought them in advance. Eight dollars if you bought them here. Joan did not realize. Digs in her bag for her wallet.

"Hey, man, she doesn't need a ticket."

She looks up. Zeke the freak. "Thanks." Sandy's elbow digs into her ribs. "Oh. This is my friend, Sandy..." she begins, but

Zeke the Freak is already heading off. Sandy gives her a pissed-off look. Joan drags out her wallet and buys Sandy a ticket. First things first. They head for the beer. It is packed in ice in a couple of big washtubs. Supposed to leave a dollar in a tin can beside the tubs. Sandy grabs a couple, shoves one in Joan's hand and pulls her off toward the crowd.

"They're trying to raise money, you know," says Joan reproachfully.

"Come on. They're raking it in."

Joan's attention is caught by the sun glinting on the big, old, green Impala pulling out of the driveway. The car the guys drive. Zeke's car. Only Elliot is driving it. Joan's heart falls, but she figures he will be back later and she will stay until he returns. In the field some guys have dragged a flatbed farm trailer near to the house. They are stringing out wires from the house and setting up amps. Other guys are unloading a keyboard and some guitars. Wow. A band. Zeke the Freak passes by again. Reaches into his pocket and pulls out a baggie. Fishes out a little, round, brown, organic-looking thing.

"Peyote. Want some?"

Joan sees herself leaping around the landscape like Carlos Castanadas. Since reading his books she has been dying to try peyote. "Yeah."

"Tastes bad, but you've got to chew it."

"Okay," she says, popping it into her mouth. He is right. It is not pleasant. After half chewing it she washes it down with beer.

"How about me?" asks Sandy.

"Sorry, man. Limited edition." Sandy glares at him. He heads off into the crowd.

Joan and Sandy wander down to the river. It wraps around the bottom of the field. The road continues past the farm, over a bridge. Getting hot, so lots of people are swimming. Four guys have stripped down to the buff. Couple of girls in nothing but panties. Mostly people just jump in with clothes on. Will not take long to dry off. Sandy spots some guy she thinks she can get drugs off. Heads in his direction. Joan sees Draino on the bridge.

Goes over to say hello. As soon as she gets there he picks her up and dumps her off the bridge into the water. Not very deep. She hits bottom kind of hard. Comes up sputtering. Draino splashes down beside her. Knocks her off her feet. Throws her over his shoulder and hauls her to the shore.

"You creep!" she spits. Checks her bag, everything is soaked. Looks like her watch made it, though. She was not under too long. "Now I don't have any butts." Holding up her sodden cigarette pack.

"Don't sweat it," he croons. "Isn't it beautiful today?" Joan gives him a dirty look and stalks off. The sun is really hot now. Kind of glad to be in damp clothes. Sprawls on the bank. Watches the nude swimmers. Joan has had few chances to see completely naked adult male bodies. A car comes by. Slows down. Horrified older farm couple gape at the sight. One of the nude guys jumps in front of the car. Waggles his dick at them. The old guy jumps out of the car. Starts yelling about youngsters today. "No sense of decency?" he screams. The nude guy laughs and jumps into the river. The old couple drives off.

Suddenly Joan's stomach starts to roll. Head spins as she staggers toward a bush. Heaves her guts out. Feels better after that. Looks up and sees some guy has been watching her. Pretty embarrassing.

"You okay?"

"Yeah." Starting to get off in fact. Moves away from the bush. Flops down.

"Want a piece of gum?" Joan is touched by his thoughtfulness. After throwing up, her mouth does taste awful. The guy sits beside her. He is a farm guy. Goes to high school in town. Couple grades below her. She does not know him that well but has heard he is neat. Everybody calls him Witch Doctor. Joan does not know why. He is chattering away about the guys in the Farmhouse.

"Got invited because they rent this place from my dad."

"Yeah?"

"Uh-huh. It's our land all around here. My dad owns seven

farms. This one here, though, is where my great-grandparents homesteaded. Neat, eh?" Joan does think it is neat. Neat to have a history where you live. To know you belong. She envies Witch Doctor.

The band is playing. Joan drifts back up the hill. Feels like she is floating. Tries to will herself to the top. If you really believe, you can do it. Then she is there. Just like Castanadas. Or maybe time is playing tricks. Did it take her hours to walk up from the river? Or a flash? Finds a shady spot under a tree. Everybody is gathering to hear the band. A soft breeze from the river relieves the heat of the sun. Small white blossoms, like confetti, are blowing off the tree. With her bandana off, her hair has curled into soft waves, now ornamented with tiny, white petals. Looks around to see if Elliot is back. Thinks he would have to fall for her if he saw her now.

The band is great! Should be making records. Joan would buy them. Perfect day. Good sign for a fine summer. Sinks back on her elbows. Eyes closed. Grooving with the music. Pretty soon she is going to have to get up to pee, maybe get a beer and bum a cig. In a minute or two. Right now she cannot move. She smells the pungent odour of fresh, male sweat. Lips are pressed against hers. Joan opens her eyes. Zeke the Freak.

"Hi, babe." Kisses her again. Joan pushes him away. "Hey, don't be like that. I have this feeling you and me could make beautiful music together." Joan cannot believe he would use a line like that. Dope. Time for that beer and cigarette. And pee. She tries to get up. He pushes her back down. Flat on her back and he is on top. She cannot breathe. Zeke weighs heavily on her chest.

"You know you want me."

Joan starts to laugh. Zeke looks hurt. "It's all these pick-up lines you're using!" Giggling. Feeling a rush of strength. She heaves him off, wills herself upright. Next she wills herself to the beer tubs. Magically finds herself there with a beer in her hand. Or did she walk over? Before she knows it she is standing in line for the washroom. All chicks. The guys just pee behind the barn.

She is flying. She bums a cigarette and tries to decide where she is going to will herself next. Wishes she could find Elliot. At least she could look for Sandy. Stands at the doorstep The sun is blinding and the music is deafening. Nobody she knows in sight.

"Pigs! Pigs!" Several people screaming at once. Zeke the Freak and Draino hurtling toward the driveway. Cherry top pulling in. Cop steps out. It is the police chief from town. His daughter is in Joan's class. Sherry. She is here at the party, like everybody else. Joan cannot hear what the cop is saying.

"It's okay, Officer," says Zeke the Freak. Loudly, feigning politeness. "Just a friendly pig roast." He emphasizes pig and chuckles. Joan is amazed at his nerve. Sherry's dad shrugs it off. Sherry appears just then, smiling. Tells her dad everything is fine. Sherry's dad opens the door to the cruiser. "Keep your clothes on and the music down," he says. The old couple who had driven by phoned in a complaint. More than anything they had objected to the naked guys.

The smell of roasting pig is everywhere. They are starting to carve meat from it. Joan wills herself to the food lineup. Not really hungry, but might as well get in line. It is a pretty long line. Lots of strangers. Joan wonders where they all came from. Lots of bikers, too. But they are behaving themselves. Joan ends up beside one tough-looking guy. Tattoos cover his forearms. Not the artistic type. These are smudgy dark grey, amateur, probably prison tattoos. Swastika. Some initials. A jagged-blade dagger. Heart split in two. Across the fingers of his left hand are the letters H.A.T.E. Across the fingers of his right hand are the letters L.O.V.E. All really crude and ugly.

He lets Joan in line in front of him. "Ladies first." Very polite and sincere. Joan is taken aback. So mean-looking, but so nice. He even goes to get her a beer when she says she is thirsty. When he gets back he lights up a reefer. Hands her a toke. Joan thinks her stone could use a touch-up. Only takes one toke, but minutes later she is really buzzing. Biker pot. Laced with something.

Nearly at the food table now. Sandy comes up and gets in line with Joan. Joan is pissed off. She has been in line fifteen minutes.

Behind her the line is snaking all the way to the back of the field now. Sandy always manages to take advantage. But with Sandy there, Joan can ditch the biker once they load up their plates.

Not many chairs. Joan and Sandy settle onto the grass. The band has stopped playing so they can eat, too. Kind of peaceful. Joan's appetite comes on strong all of a sudden. The food tastes absolutely delicious. Heavenly. Joan is really getting into eating. Then Sandy starts screaming, throws her plate down.

"Get them off me! Get them off me!" Thinks bugs are crawling all over her. Joan knows she did acid. Sandy always thinks she has bugs crawling on her when she does acid. She is thrashing around. Some guys they know grab her and restrain her. It takes a while for her to settle down. The guys say they are going back to town if she wants a ride. Sandy takes it.

Joan looks around to see if Elliot has come back. Does not see him. Decides to will herself to where he is. Finds herself instantly transported to the beer tubs. Bums a cigarette from Zeke the Freak. The sun is down now. Getting cold. Draino is organizing a bonfire. There is a procession of bikers carrying piles of dead branches from the woodlot behind the barn. Not long before flames are licking the sky. Cannot get very close. The front of Joan's body is searing hot. Her back is covered in goose pimples. The polite biker is beside her again. Says he can warm her up. Zeke the Freak is on her other side. He puts his arms around her and the biker moves off. Joan is relieved. Zeke the Freak is smiling.

The band has left. Just one guy on the flatbed, fooling around on a guitar. Fire dying down. Getting late. People are ambling down the driveway. The sound of a car starting and pulling away is repeated every few minutes. Tail lights disappearing over the hill. Joan is chilled. Should leave soon, but she is still looking forward to seeing Elliot. The bikers leave en masse. Almost nobody left now. The party is over. Zeke the Freak steers her toward the Farmhouse.

"Got something to show you." Leads her up the stairs.

"Oh, yeah. Like your bed."

"No, no, no!" Zeke looks offended.

"Okay, what?"

At the end of the hall upstairs is a gun rack. Seven or eight rifles lined up neatly.

"My gun collection." Proud.

Joan grimaces. Cannot believe it. Like some kind of redneck, she thinks. Zeke the Freak grabs one of the rifles and drags her back downstairs and out onto the porch.

"Try firing it."

"What?"

"Go ahead, give it a try."

After some convincing he is showing her how to hold it properly.

"Just point it into the bush."

She cocks it. Squeezes the trigger. Blam. Huge explosion. Joan is propelled backward. Nearly falls over, but regains her balance. Zeke the Freak is looking at her with new-found admiration.

"Man, I thought that would knock you on your ass. That there is the equivalent of an elephant gun!" Her shoulder is aching. It dawns on her that her hip is throbbing with pain, too. Then she remembers hitting bottom when Draino threw her in the river. She is angry that Zeke the Freak tried to make a fool out of her with the gun.

There is rustling and yelling in the bush. Draino and Sherry, the police chief's daughter, come fighting their way through the underbrush. "Hey, man. You trying to kill someone?"

Suddenly Joan is completely straight. Kind of numb feeling. Draino swears he felt the wind from the bullet whiz by his head. Good thing they were both lying down. Laughs at the thought of the police chief finding their bodies in the position they were in. Sherry giggles. Joan looks at her watch. Wishes she could will herself back to town. The magic has worn off. She offers Sherry a ride. Zeke the Freak looks disappointed. Then she remembers.

"What happened to Elliot tonight?"

Zeke the Freak looks even more crestfallen. "Hey, man. You really like him, don't you?"

"Just wondering."

"Oh, well. He left for out west. Lots of money to be made out there. Oil business."

"I saw him leaving in your car."

"Yeah, I sold it to him. Bought a bike for the summer. Sucker paid me way too much for that heap."

beach bonfire

Saturday morning. 7:30 a.m. Phone rings. Joan's mom yells up the stairs. It's for Sandy.

"Get the hell over here." Joan can hear Laidie on the other end. Sandy's mother. Steaming mad.

Sandy hangs up. "I'm supposed to be helping my mother paint one of the cottages."

Joan groans. "All right. See you later." Now she knows why Sandy wanted to sleep over. Thought she could get out of painting this morning.

"So. Are you coming?" asks Sandy.

"No way. I have to work the dinner shift and there's the dance tonight."

Somehow Joan ends up heading over to Sandy's. Pissed off at herself for giving in. Never wins with Sandy. It's early, the streets are deserted. Sun is already hot. Blinding. Joan squints. They are crossing the main street. The one car on the road this morning swings around the corner. Forces them to break into a trot. Suddenly two guys are in front of them. Blocking the way. Right in the middle of the intersection.

"Hey, girls. Where's the action in this town?"

"Dry up and blow away." Joan spits.

The guys look at each other. They back off. Skirt around Joan. Sandy grabs Joan's arm.

"What are you, crazy? Did you see those guys?"

Joan looks over her shoulder. They look alright. Tall, good-looking, great clothes and haircuts. Excellent, in fact. Joan feels a pang.

"Yeah, well, I'm in a bad mood," she snaps. Still, she is kicking herself about the guys. At the same time happy to get back at Sandy for dragging her out this morning.

Sandy does not talk the rest of the way. She does not say a word until they have been painting for about an hour. Laidie hands over the paint and leaves them to it. Joan spends several hours helping Sandy paint the cottage, which is going to be vacant for a couple of days. Sandy's mom rents these housekeeping cottages during the summer. Six tiny brown and yellow cabins tucked into a shady lot behind Sandy's house. They are usually booked solid all summer long. Sometimes obnoxious families, sometimes cool guys. You never know. Except the regulars. For instance, the same two weeks every summer this girl, Karen, comes with her parents from London, Ontario. She is the same age as Sandy and Joan. They have a great time with Karen.

In winter Sandy's mom is a teacher. She is also the first local girl to get a divorce. Big scandal. Kind of ironic. Two weeks after the divorce came through Sandy's father was killed. Snowmobiling. Head neatly severed by a wire fence he did not see.

The sun gets hotter. Painting is gruelling. It would have taken Sandy all day if it was not for Joan helping. They have a few breaks. Laugh at the sloppy job they are doing. By the end of the morning Joan and Sandy are friends again.

"Meet you at the Cabana after work."

"Okay."

Joan has just enough time to have a bit of a rest and get cleaned up for work. It is a pretty heavy dinner hour. One of those nights where you do not even get to clear a table before somebody sits down at it. Big tables, too. Lots of families. Impatient. With picky, snotty little kids. Tourist season has started for sure. Joan is worn out. Does not think she will go to the dance after all. The walk home calms her down, though. Getting dressed and made up brings back her energy. Excited. First dance of the summer at the Cabana.

The Cabana is an old forties dance hall. Towns all up and down the lakeshore had them. One by one they have been closing down. The Cabana still rocks. Sandy's mom remembers big bands there in the fifties. Every summer the Cabana is packed for rock dances on Thursday, Friday, and Saturday nights. There are Sunday midnight dances on long weekends. The old forties decor is cool. High sloping roof with wooden rafters hung with streamers. Big parquet dance floor. Mirror ball hangs over the centre. Outdoor patio with wicker furniture. Every weekend a different band's bus parked outside. Painted in neat colours, usually some kind of funky mural.

Joan sees Sandy near the front of the line. Great, she won't have to wait long. Squeezes in. Sandy pulls out a spliff.

"Good stuff. Got it from a biker."

Three, maybe four tokes. Joan is already feeling it.

"The guy said he doctored it with oil."

"Maybe something else, too," says Joan. She can't believe how high she is already.

Sandy goes in first and fights her way to the front of the stage. Next thing she is back beside Joan, dragging her to the stage. Shooting daggers with her eyes.

"Take a look."

Joan looks at the band. It is the guys from this morning. The lead singer and the lead guitarist. Joan and Sandy have long dreamed of meeting guys from one of the bands. They have spent hours scheming about how to do it. Joan blew their chance to live out the fantasy of every girl in town.

"Jesus Christ, Joan, why are you always such a snob with guys?" Joan doesn't know what to say. Sandy goes stomping off. Joan heads over to the snack bar. Major case of the munchies. She gets a large fries and a Coke.

"Watch out for the bikers tonight," says Stan the Man, who is working behind the counter tonight. Self-appointed bodyguard to the entire student body of the high school. Big guy. Not just tall, but broad. Football player. Such a greaser, and does not even realize how goofy he is. "I think it's the Hell's Angels," he says with annoying self-assurance. Joan nods and moves off. Finds a table, wolfs down her fries. The band is really great. Joan is feeling pretty regretful. She also would really like to dance. Scans the crowd. Doesn't see anybody likely.

Oh, no. Zeke the Freak. Still will not leave her alone. Been bugging her ever since the pig roast. Now that Elliot took off out west she is not much interested in hanging around Zeke and Draino. Stuck with this maniac and does not know how to get rid of him. He has got some kind of fantasy or obsession about her. Always coming up with dorky lines he thinks she will fall for. If she dances with him, she will not be able to get rid of him for the rest of the night. Takes off in the opposite direction. Too late.

"Hey, Joan!" Pretends she doesn't see him. "Hey, Joan, wait up! Joan, you look beautiful tonight." Joan waves ahead of her, at nobody. Hopes he will think she is meeting somebody. "Hey, Joan." Piercing scream just as the music lets up. "You look like a *Vogue* model!" Joan's cheeks burn. People are looking at her. She ducks into the crowd. Looks over her shoulder, sees him walking past. Great. She's lost him. Keeps pushing through the crowd. Then there is this foul smell. It's like an outhouse or something. Joan gags and covers her nose.

"Pretty bad, eh?" Linda, a girl who just graduated from grade 13, is beside her. Joan is a bit staggered. Linda. Speaking to her. Linda was the prom queen this year and goes out with one of the foxiest guys in town. Martin, the minister's son.

"Yeah, what is it?" Trying to sound nonchalant.

"Some bike gang. They brought a bunch of new guys. Their initiation was that all the members of the gang pissed on them. Now they have to walk around for a week without washing or changing their clothes."

"Oh, yeah? That's gross." Joan is feeling a bit woozy. That spliff. She wished she had not taken so many tokes. "I'm going out for some fresh air."

"I'll come with you."

Joan glides on air going out of the Cabana beside Linda.

Looks around. Sees Sandy. Gives her a smirk. Sandy gives her the finger. Joan does not care. There must be fifty bikes parked outside. Bikers milling everywhere. Joan and Linda skirt the crowd and head for the harbour. Out on the breakwall it is cool and dark. Joan's head is starting to clear. A few couples are out here going at it hot and heavy. Got to watch you do not trip over them. The beach, the harbour, and the breakwall form a U. Out at the end of the breakwall they are directly across from the Cabana. The music drifts across the water.

"Fucking bikers," says Linda. "I really wanted to dance. It's a good band, but I can't stay in there."

"Yeah, it is a good band." Joan tells her the story about meeting the guys in the morning.

"Bummer," says Linda. "Was that Zeke running after you in there?"

"Yeah. Zeke the Freak. So embarassing."

"He's got good stuff."

"True."

"Hey, I got a spliff off some bikers. Want a toke?"

Oh, no, thinks Joan. Then she realizes she is not so stoned anymore. "Okay."

The same stuff that Sandy had. Joan is careful to take only a couple of tokes. Linda is telling her all sorts of things about Martin, the minister's son. Giggling. Joan cannot believe what she is hearing. Linda lost her virginity in the church. Some kind of ceremony that Martin came up with. Black candles, upside-down cross. He read about it in some book. A couple months later Martin stole from the collection box to pay for an abortion. Wait until Sandy hears. No. Fuck Sandy.

"Don't tell anyone I told you this. Marty'll kill me." Linda has let her mouth get ahead of her brain. "He wants to get into law school."

Now they are suddenly aware that the music has stopped. Joan and Linda look across the water to the Cabana. Their jaws drop. Almost simultaneously every door in the building bursts open and people come pouring out. Some running. Some in rolling brawls. The beach is a riot scene. Police cars screech from every direction. Not just cops from town. Oinkers from all the nearby towns. Joan sees a bunch of bikers swarm a cruiser, ripping off the doors and smashing the cherry. Well, fuck a duck.

"Wow, let's go!" says Linda.

"Um. I can't move." Speaking is a painful effort.

Pause. "Me neither."

They both fall silent. Watching. Wide-eyed. No sign of action subsiding. Then it is too weird. Flames are licking through the roof of the Cabana. Smoke is pouring from the outside order window of the snack shop. More people running from the building. Does not take long before the old wooden structure is like one tremendous beach bonfire. The town fire siren is sounding for the volunteers to come. It is half an hour before the town's two fire engines make it to the beach. Not much they can do. Flames shoot high into the sky under a plume of dark, dark smoke. The Cabana's roof starts to crash in. Finally it all just collapses. Whumph. All the firemen can do is keep people from getting too close. The fighting has stopped. Everybody is just watching.

Joan and Linda still cannot move. At least there is lots to see from where they are sitting. So why bother? After a while Zeke's friend Draino comes strolling out the breakwall. Sits beside them.

"Good view from here." He looks at Joan. "Woman, Zeke's been looking for you all night. He's been worried."

"Can't move."

"Oh, yeah? You toke any of that bikers' spliff?"

"Yeah."

"Angel dust." Draino gets up. Salutes them good-bye. "Stick to Zeke's stuff, woman. You don't know what you're gonna get from a biker."

Four in the morning. Dew falling on them. Shivering. They have to force every muscle in their bodies to move. They make it to the beach. A few people still watching as the fire department wets down the embers. Somebody offers them a ride home.

Joan thinks, "When I wake up I will be straight." It is her only straw to grasp.

She wakes up stoned. Lies in bed for hours. Wide awake. Still cannot move. Miserable. Thinking about the guys in the band. Which one would she have gotten? Sandy always gets the best. Second-best of those two would still be okay. Maybe they could have taken off for the summer in the band's bus. Stopping at all the cool bars and resorts. They could hang around the band room at the Cabana the next time the band came to town. Except the Cabana is gone. Very sad. Joan would like to cry but she feels like some sort of cold reptile. She has got to get up. Supposed to be at work for four o'clock again today. If she gets moving and has something to eat, the stone will go away. She hopes.

Nope. After fumbling in the kitchen and making a huge mess she still has not achieved any kind of meal. Decides to go in early and eat at work. Cannot even walk. Takes the car. Sits at the coffee counter and has a hamburger. Ravenously hungry, but sickened by the food. Wonders how she is going to be able to work.

Sandy comes in with Zeke the Freak and Draino. They laugh at the way she looks.

"How come you're not in this kind of shape?" Joan asks Sandy.

"Guess I knew when to stop."

"Yeah, she lost her spliff," sniggers Draino. Sandy, Zeke, and Draino left the beach together after the fire. Sandy sneaked Zeke and Draino into the empty cottage for the night. Saved them a trip out to their farmhouse. Two guys on a bike on that winding road. Could have been bad. Everybody had toked a little angel dust before they figured out what it was.

"Pheew, and the paint fumes didn't help," says Zeke. Sandy giggles. Dull stab to Joan's reptilian heart. Did Sandy and Zeke...? Come on. No reason to be jealous.

"So, what happened last night?" Joan asks.

"The Cabana burned down." More giggling. Very funny.

"Yeah, yeah. I watched it all. I mean how?"

"Well, the Cabana owners tried to get the stinking bikers to leave. So the bikers started to push and shove. So asshole Stan the Man jumped over the snack counter to throw his weight around. All hell broke loose. Everybody going crazy...."

"Yeah, I saw that."

"So, Stan the Man forgets about the chip fryer. That's where the fire started. The whole snack shop was up in flames before anybody realized. They were too busy fighting."

"Stan the Man. What an asshole."

"No more Cabana." Silence. No place to dance. No place to meet guys. No place to score drugs.

"So, which section is yours? We thought we'd be your first table tonight."

Angel dust. Sounds heavenly. This was not heaven. Every movement Joan had to make was like pushing against a wall. Each and every muscle action required intense concentration. The steak house was packed, with a lineup out the door. Cold hatred filled Joan's heart for every hopeful face waiting for a meal.

"Fucking rich city jerks. Don't they have kitchens in their cottages?" she thought.

She left people sitting at dirty tables. Ignored their pleading eyes. Did her job like a zombie. Every time she passed Sandy, Zeke, and Draino's table they laughed out loud. Biggest joke of the year.

"Ha, ha, ha." Sandy's loud, half-spoken laugh cut through the noise of the other diners. Joan could even hear it when she was in the kitchen. Sandy, Zeke, and Draino stayed forever. Coffee. Dessert. More coffee. How about another beer? One sweet vindication. Joan had to tell the bartender to refuse to serve Sandy alcohol. Knowing her age.

"Liquor inspector could be in any moment. I'm not paying the fine."

More guffaws. Joan sniffs and walks away. Sandy can have her laughs. She can have Zeke. Nothing they do can bug her.

Finally they leave. But that does not make working any easier. Still a living hell. Joan's shift is from four to ten. About nine o'clock the weights drop from her limbs. She realizes the stone is over at last. That is when she sits down in the middle of the floor and starts bawling her eyes out.

passing through

Not too hot yet. Late morning. Good to lie in the sun. Slight breeze off the water. Joan and Sandy partied pretty heavy last night. They are wasted. Even so, it is worth the effort to come down to the beach. Beautiful day. Clear. Intense colours. Sand sparkling like diamonds. In a few minutes Joan will be hot enough to go for a dip. The lake is still pretty cold. Does not really warm up until the end of July. But if you get really hot it is great.

Sandy is already turning deep brown. Joan curses her own fair complexion. Always ends up burning herself to a crisp trying to get a tan. Painful for a couple of days. Tan for a couple of days. After two day shifts at the steak house it is back to square one. Has to stay out in the sun every day to maintain her tan. Even then the best she can do is a kind of a wishy-washy beige. During the summer Joan feels like a piebald pony. Different parts of her body are different colours at different times. Parts tanned, parts burned, patches of peeling skin, and other parts that never tan and always stay white. The worst is her tummy. Glows in the dark. Combine that with a little padding of baby fat. Makes for less than sexy bikini-wearing. Maybe time to turn over and fry her belly for a while.

She hears the whining of a motorcycle engine. It is coming closer. What the fuck? Joan and Sandy look up in time for this Kawasaki to drive right between them. Right up onto their beach blanket. The guy driving is kind of cute. Wearing jeans and a T-shirt, jean jacket, mirrored aviator glasses. Not a gang rider. Joan and Sandy do not move. Look at each other, look at the guy on the Kawi.

"Saw the two best-looking asses on the beach. Had to say hello," says the guy.

Joan and Sandy look around. It's a weekday. It's early in the day. The beach is pretty much deserted.

"There is nobody else on the beach," says Joan.

"Still pretty good-looking asses," says the guy.

Joan does not reply. Sandy jumps up and starts inspecting the bike. The guy did his own custom paint job. Sandy oohs and aahs. Joan sits up to take a look.

"Want a ride, long legs?" Looking at Joan.

Really obsessed with body parts. "Aren't you going to finish analyzing the rest of my body first?"

"Oohh, she's bitchy, too. Want a ride?"

Joan gets on. Sits casually behind the guy. Tries to make out like she's on bikes all the time. He shoots off. Fishtailing a bit on the sand. Joan's heart rises into her throat. Clutches the guy's jacket a little tighter. Hugs the seat with her thighs. Doing her best to look nonchalant. This guy will be impressed if she shows him how tough she is. He goes faster and faster. There are a couple of times, going around corners, when Joan thinks she is going to die. All she has on is her bikini. Sees herself skidding along the pavement. Flesh shredding off her bones. Finally he turns back toward the beach. Delivers her to the blanket where Sandy is waiting.

"This chick has nerves of steel," he says. Joan beams. The guy offers Sandy a ride. They take off. Joan lies down on her back. Going to get her tummy tanned. Being out and about on a motorcycle could be good for her tan. Sees herself in a bikini top and cut-offs whizzing around town. Waving to friends. Everybody would ask who he was. How did they meet? Drove right up on my beach blanket, she would say.

"Ha, ha, ha." Joan hears Sandy's laugh over the wail of the

engine. They are back down on the beach. The guy is doing doughnuts in the sand. After a while he pulls the bike up to the beach blanket. Sandy's arms are wrapped tightly around his waist. Head resting on his back. Thighs clenched on his hips. Joan laughs.

"He's a maniac!" screams Sandy. Giggling.

"Couldn't go fast enough to get a hug from *her*," he says, nodding toward Joan. "I was speeding like crazy and she's still sitting there cool as a cucumber." He lifts Sandy off the bike and gives her a hug. "So, I'll pick you up around eight o'clock?" Smile disappears from Joan's face. She and Sandy watch as the guy drives off.

"I think he liked you better. But, as usual, you had to be so cold and bitchy," says Sandy. She's right. Once again. Joan has totally misjudged the situation. Why is she so dumb about guys? She gets up. Gathers her things. Heads home.

"There was a boy here asking for you," says her mother. Joan is surprised she is home. Not at her father's office. Her parents' office. Her father is a lawyer and her mother works as his secretary.

"Mrs. Alexander's funeral today," says her mother in explanation. Knowing the question in Joan's head before she can ask it. "The fellow's name was Zeke." Pause. "You know, I don't think I like his brand of cigarettes." Joan rolls her eyes. Her mother has liked to show off how she can recognize the smell of pot ever since she did that little seminar at the police department. No doubt Zeke the Freak reeked of it. Joan cannot believe he came to her house. She is going to have to find a boyfriend fast to get him off her back.

"You know, if you go down to the harbour you can probably meet lots of young men. I've noticed quite a few boys in your age group on the yachts comings through. They're travelling with their families, so you know they are going to be nice. And their families have money if they can afford a yacht."

Joan sighs and goes up the stairs to her room. "You can fall in love with a rich man as easily as you can with a poor man," her mother yells up the stairs after her.

Joan meets Sandy at the beach again the next day.

"So. I did it," says Sandy.

"Did what?"

"You know."

"No!"

"Yes."

"With Mr. Body Parts?" Joan cannot keep the sarcasm out of her voice.

"Don't be such a snob. You're just jealous. He's really cute and nice. He has some killer hash. Went to his campsite at the KOA. Just sat around the fire and got totally ripped. Then we just started kissing. Wow, it was unbelievable." Sandy goes on breathlessly describing everything in detail. "Kind of sore, though." Sandy is extremely satisfied. Losing her virginity. The goal she had set for herself this summer. Sandy's little sister Julie did it already. Julie had been seeing this guy, Scott, for a long time. Ever since she was twelve. Over the winter Julie told Sandy she did it with Scott in his uncle's barn. Drove Sandy wild to think Julie had beat her to it.

Joan thought it was going to happen with Elliot. She went to a gynecologist in Owen Sound. Told him about her bad period cramps. Got put on the pill. Been on for a couple of months. It is really helping with her period cramps. Not much need for it otherwise.

"This is our lucky day! The two neatest chicks in town." Zeke the Freak and Draino approaching across the sand. They drop into squats at the end of the blanket. Zeke pulls out a doob. "Want a toke?"

Sandy sits up immediately. All smiles. Sandy, Zeke, and

Draino have been hanging around a bit. Bummer for Joan. Harder to avoid Zeke. Three of them are getting all giggly. Joan is not toking. She lies face-down, ignoring the others. Then Zeke's face is right in hers. Lying down alongside her. Smiling. She sits up with a frown.

"Hey, there was nothing with Sandy and me that night," he says. "When I stayed in her cabin after the Cabana burnt down."

"I know."

"We were all too high. Besides, I'm not interested in Sandy…."

"I know." Cutting him off. "She already told me!" Like she even cared. The other two are staring at them now. "So, Zeke, have you heard anything from Elliot?"

Zeke gets a pissed-off look on his face. Joan smiles to herself. "That guy is a real freak, Joan. You don't want to know."

"Maybe I would," she says. Zeke is silent.

"Hey. You chicks coming to our party Saturday night?" Draino sticks his head in.

"Yeah. At the Farmhouse?" Sandy brimming with enthusiasm.

"Yup. Going to be a major bash," assures Draino.

"Can I bring a new guy I just met?" Asks Sandy.

"Oh sure, the more the merrier."

Joan sits on a bench at the side of the harbour. Eating an ice cream. Warm, soft evening. After work she came down to the beach. Pearly, mauve sky reflected in the water. Lots of boats in the harbour tonight. Lots of people ambling, eating ice cream. Looking at yachts. Watching the sunset.

A guy sits down beside her. Clean-cut. White tennis shorts, tank top, topsiders. Brown, muscular, compact body. "Which boat you on?" he asks.

"I'm from town."

"Really? A local girl?"

"Yes." Is that so remarkable?

"I've been cruising with my parents for a couple of weeks now and I haven't met any locals at any of the ports so far."

"Don't get too excited."

"No, no. It's just neat. I'm sick of all these yacht people."

"Why?"

"I don't know, I just am. Want to come see my dad's boat?"

"Sure."

This boat is too fucking incredible. Living room bigger than the one at Joan's home. Big button tuft bar. The guy gets out some gin and tonic. Mixes up a couple of drinks. Twist of lemon and everything. Classy. All the guys Joan knows only drink beer. Maybe rye and Coke once in a while. Joan settles into a deep leather couch. Trying to look sophisticated.

"My name is Rich," says the guy.

"Are you kidding?" Joan laughs.

"What?"

"Well...your name...I mean..." Waves her arm at the opulence around her.

"Oh, yeah, I guess I never thought of it that way." Snickers.

Joan giggles. "I'm going to call you Richie Rich."

"Oh, here are my parents.... Hi, mom. Hi, Dad." Cheerful. Like he's actually glad to see them.

The parents fill the room, big as it is. Mrs. Rich glides in surrounded by a solid force field of perfume. Mr. Rich has a voice and a laugh that resounds off the walls. They make a big fuss over Joan. "What a lovely girl. It's late. You better walk her home."

They walk and they talk. Rich delivers her to her front door.

"We're here until Sunday. Do you want to see a movie or something tomorrow?"

Tomorrow is Friday. She has a lunch shift at the steak house, but nothing planned for the evening. "Yeah, that would be fun."

Joan's mother gets to the door before Joan can. Richie Rich

has brought flowers! Joan always thought that was something that only happened on TV. He is wearing jeans and a denim shirt, exactly matched in colour. Pressed. Not a frayed thread. Not a hair out of place on his head. Polished brown loafers. Belt the same colour of brown. Joan's mother beams. Joan looks down at what she had decided to wear.

"I'll just get changed," she says, suddenly embarrassed by what she had thought were cool clothes. Puts on the unfaded, unfrayed jeans and floral blouse she wears when she goes to visit her grandparents. Hopes she does not run into too many people she knows.

The movie is fine. Most kids go to every new film that comes to town, no matter what it is. The show changes once a week, on Wednesday. Everybody goes that night. Joan missed it this week, so she is happy to be going tonight. Rich buys her a large pop, a large popcorn, and a chocolate bar. Her own. Guys around here usually get stuff to share. He holds her hand lightly. Lets his shoulder touch hers. That is it. Even during the sexy part he does not grope her.

Walks her straight home. "Can I see you again tomorrow night?"

Bash at Zeke's and Draino's tomorrow. Going to be pretty raunchy. "I've got a party I'm going to."

Rich's face falls. "Oh. You're already going with someone?"

"No." Pause. Thinking. Well fine. It would be one way to take care of Zeke. Normally she would drive out with Sandy. Has not seen Sandy much since Mr. Body Parts has been around. "Okay. I have to work until eight. You've got to drive to get there. I'll pick you up at the harbour. Around nine."

"Great. Can I have a kiss?" Wow. A guy who asks first. Gives her a little peck. On the cheek.

Joan is not sure which is worse. Embarrassment she feels at

what her friends must think of Richie Rich. Embarrassment she feels at what Richie Rich thinks of her friends. First of all, the bottle he pulls out of the LCBO bag he brought with him turns out to be sherry. Presents it to Zeke the Freak. Like a hostess gift her mother would take out to an evening of bridge. Zeke does not know what to do with it. Richie Rich is looking for sherry glasses. Finally Zeke just gives him a beer. Says he will save the sherry for another time. Keeps a straight face, but Joan can tell Zeke the Freak is sniggering inside. She stands close to Rich. Smiles at him. Determined to get Zeke off her back no matter what it takes.

Party is raunchy all right. Crowded. Spilling out into the yard. Some bikers show up. One biker chick does some topless dancing on the picnic table outside. Then she offers every guy in the place a blow job. Starting with Richie Rich. Rich politely declines. She moves on to the next guy. One of the bikers. Lays him down on the grass. Straddles him. Peels open his fly. Her bum is up in the air. Cut-off shorts sheared off to the seam at the crotch. Not much but the seam left. Pubes and labia hanging out. Bum pulsing back and forth as she enthusiastically sucks the biker off.

Rich takes Joan's hand. "Maybe we should go inside."

In the kitchen Sandy has just arrived.

"Where's Mr. Body Parts?"

"He's coming."

"This is my friend, Richie Rich."

Sandy is not perturbed by Rich's straight appearance. Looks like she is already pretty high. Pretty gabby. Starts asking Rich where he is from and all that. Joan looks across the kitchen and sees Linda, the prom queen, standing beside Zeke. Pretty close. All smiles. Joan leaves Sandy and Rich talking. Pushes through the crowd.

"Hey, where is Marty tonight?" It is odd to see her out at a party without Martin, the minister's son.

Linda grabs Joan's hand. Whispers, conspiratorially. "I gotta show you something. Let's go to the can." Turns to Zeke. "Be right back." Linda drags Joan upstairs. Big lineup at the bathroom. Linda opens the door to a darkened bedroom. Couple of faces caught in the glare of the hall light. Naked bodies. Biker guy and some chick. "Fuck off," says the guy. Linda slams the door. Tries the next door. Nobody there. Linda pulls Joan inside. Shuts the door. Unbuttons her blouse. Pulls it aside to show her right boob. Joan starts to back away. Then she sees. The boob is criss-crossed with tiny red welts.

"For fuck's sake," Joan whispers, "what happened?"

"Marty." Holy shit. "Don't tell anybody. He tied me down on the bed. Said he saw some movie. Some special sex trick that was supposed to be really a gas for women. So I'm helpless on this bed and he takes out this razor blade. Cut up both my tits. Like really slowly, carefully. I'm screaming and he's telling me I'm supposed to like it. Then he fucks me. Everything was covered in blood. It was so gross. Anyway, I'm finished with Marty."

Joan nods. Stunned. Not just by Linda's story. Also...why has Linda started to take Joan into her confidence?

"So, who's the guy you're with tonight?" asks Linda. "He's so cute."

"He's okay. I met him at the harbour. He's on one of the boats."

"Neat. So he's rich."

Joan chuckles. "Yeah, his name is Rich." They giggle. "He took me out last night. He brought me flowers." Joan says this as if it is some sort of deviant behavior. Still cannot get over it. Does not mention the bottle of sherry.

"Wow," says Linda. "So you're not going out with Zeke anymore."

"Never was." Perturbed that anybody may have gotten that impression.

"Oh, I thought you were since I see you together all the time. Okay, so it would be alright if I went out with him."

"Be my guest."

"Cool. He's such a neat guy."

Joan shrugs. Smiles at Linda. Goes back downstairs. "Ha, ha, ha" she hears rising above the din of the party. Sandy's laugh.

Sandy is still yakking with Richie Rich. They seem to be getting along great. Rich puts an arm around Joan's shoulder. When Rich is not looking, Sandy gives Joan the signal of approval.

"Hey, let's go outside for some fresh air," says Sandy. They fight their way to the door. Outside Sandy directs them to a quiet spot down by the river. The moon is bright. Dazzling reflection on the water. Crickets chirping loudly.

"This was a great idea," says Rich. "It's much nicer out here."

"Look what I got," says Sandy. "It's that killer hash I was telling you about." She has a major-sized chunk.

"From Mr. Body Parts?"

"Yeah."

"Let's go," says Rich. His body has stiffened and his voice has grown cold. He starts to haul Joan away. "You seem like such a nice girl," he says over his shoulder to Sandy. "I would have never thought you'd be involved with drugs."

Joan drives Rich back to town. She thinks she can go back to the party after she drops Rich off at the harbour. He will not get out of the car. Wants to talk. Mostly lecture. Joan does not say much. Amazed. She knew there were kids who did not do drugs. Always thought it was because they never had the chance.

Sunday. Rich and his parents left in the morning. After church. Walked up from the harbour for the service. Given by Martin's father. On the way back down they stop at Joan's house to say good-bye. Mr. and Mrs. Rich wave from the sidewalk. Rich comes up to the porch. Gives Joan a peck on the cheek. Asks if he can write. "Sure," says Joan. Knows she will not write back.

Later, Joan is on the beach. Belly up. Getting her tummy tanned. Towel over her face. No, Mom, she thinks, it's not as easy to fall in love with a rich man. Sighs. Thinks of Elliot. Cannot stop thinking about Elliot.

"You've got to drive me to the KOA." Joan sits up, squinting in the sun. Sandy is standing over her.

"Going to see Mr. Body Parts?"

"Going to give him hell. He never showed up at the party last night. I waited until everybody was gone. Couldn't get a ride. Had to sleep on the couch."

"Okay, let's go."

They walk up to Joan's to get the car and drive out to the KOA. No Mr. Body Parts. Campsite deserted. Sandy has a fit.

"So, what did you expect? A guy on a bike, staying at the KOA."

"He said he was going to stay for the summer, now that he met me."

"Maybe he'll be back."

"No, I don't think so."

"Where is he from?"

"Hamilton, I think."

"So, call information, get his number."

Sandy sits down. Kind of slumps. "I never got his name," she sighs.

penis butter

Sitting in a booth at the steak house coffee shop. Joan has just finished the morning shift. Changed out of her uniform. She is having fries and a Coke with Sandy. Joan is looking forward to an evening off. Took another girl's evening shift this week and she has been working eight days straight. And tomorrow is her day off. The show is changing at the cinema tonight. Looks like it's going to be a pretty good movie. Joan is planning to go. Everybody will be there. When the show changes on Wednesdays everybody goes.

The coffee shop is deserted except for Joan and Sandy. It is midafternoon, the lunch crowd has gone. Sitting at the back, looking down the long aisle between the counter and the row of booths. Bright sun outside barely filters back to them through the tangled and scruffy-looking plants crowding the front window.

"Sure is hot out there," says Sandy. Joan is cold. Air conditioner rattling away over the door. When it's busy and Joan is running she is thankful for the air conditioning. The rest of the time Joan spends shivering. No sweaters are allowed. Spoils the look of the uniforms. Joan would like to get out into the heat and spend some time on the beach. Sandy is in no hurry. Wants to cool off a bit before going back out. Worked up a sweat this morning cleaning cottages for her mother. Sandy finishes her fries, sits back, lights up a cigarette. Joan decides she might as well pour herself a coffee. Other than the no-sweater shit, her bosses are pretty good. No problem with sitting around snacking after work. Steve, the cook, even treated Sandy to fries today. Double-fried, extra brown and crispy. Slow lunch. Lots left over.

Front door jingles. Some guy standing at the cash. Cannot make out who it is because he is in silhouette. Looks like he just wants to buy cigarettes. The Greeks are all busy in the kitchen so Joan goes up to serve him. It is Martin, the minister's son.

"Hi, Joan." She is surprised he knows her name. He usually hangs around with a group of snooty grade thirteeners. Joan did not think they ever paid any attention to anyone outside their circle. Soooo sophisticated. Must have started to notice her because she has been hanging around with Linda.

"I'll take a pack of Export A," he says. She slaps the pack on the counter. He puts down the money. Glances at Sandy sitting in the back booth. "I could use a coffee. Mind if I join you girls?"

Sandy's head snaps around. Before Joan can say anything Sandy has invited Martin to sit with them. Joan gets him a coffee on her way back to the booth. Not sure she wants to sit with him. Not after what Linda says he did to her. Sandy is visibly excited. Joan knows that Sandy has always thought Martin is super-cute. He is going off to Queen's in the fall. So neat. Martin sits where Joan had been sitting. When she gets to the booth he scoots over so she can sit down. She picks up her coffee and sits on Sandy's side of the booth, pushing Sandy into the corner.

Martin and Sandy start yakking away. Joan is getting impatient. Wants to get to the beach. It's almost 3:00. She is missing the strongest sun of the day. Been practically living in the coffee shop and dining lounge at the steak house for over a week. Her tan has faded to nothing. And she's freezing. Cannot wait to get out and start frying herself in the sun.

"How about going to the movie tonight?" Martin is talking to her. Joan looks up.

"Um. We've got this family dinner thing." It is what Joan always says when she wants to get out of a date. Not a lie. Her mother insists on making every dinner a family thing. Not that she would not be free later on. Shit, though. Now she will not be able to go to the movie. Can go tomorrow, but that is not "the" night when everybody goes to the movie. Oh, well.

"So, how about you?" He asks Sandy. Joan thinks Sandy is going to cream her jeans.

"Oh, yeah! They say it's going to be the best movie of the summer!"

"Okay, let's go to the late show. I'll meet you at the stoplights around eight-thirty." He takes off.

Joan is thinking maybe she can go to the early show and sneak out without them seeing her.

"Now all I have to do is find somebody to babysit for Cathy tonight." Sandy's other source of income is sitting for Cathy pretty regularly. Other than helping her mother with the cottages.

"I'll do it."

Sandy stares at Joan. "I thought you had some family thing."

"No. I just did not want to go to the movie with Martin."

"Why not?"

Joan promised Linda she would not tell anybody about Martin's weird stuff. Sandy could get hurt, though. Joan thinks of Linda's scarred breasts. But everybody in town would know by tomorrow if she told Sandy. Linda would kill her.

"I don't think it's a good idea to go out with Martin."

"Just because you're friends with Linda now." A sore spot for Sandy. Sandy is jealous. Joan is now hanging around with some grade thirteeners. Kids who will be going into college in the fall. But so far Sandy has not been welcomed into the group. "I'm going to the movie with Martin."

"You want to know why Linda broke off with him…?" Joan starts.

"I bet it was him that left her and now she's telling stories about him," snapped Sandy. Determined.

"Okay, okay. What time am I supposed to be at Cathy's?"

✸

Cathy is Sandy's second or third cousin. Something like that. Sandy is related to practically everybody in town. When Joan first moved to town and met Sandy, she was amazed that Sandy introduced almost everbody as a cousin. Or an aunt. Or an uncle. Joan's cousins are all far away. Later on, when she got to know more people, she realized the whole population of the town was interrelated in some way. More than ten years later Joan is still a new girl in town. Her father is the new lawyer. The sign by his door still has the name of the old guy. The guy who was the lawyer for about a hundred years before her father came. Her dad partnered with the old guy until he died. People still come in to the office asking for the old guy. Dead now for about six years.

Cathy is married to Jack. Jack who is the mechanic at the Esso. Jack is also Sandy's cousin, only on her father's side. Sort of a Romeo and Juliet thing because the two sides of the family hated each other after Sandy's parents divorced. Sandy thought Cathy was so neat because of this. Also, Cathy let Sandy help herself to the liquor cabinet and take packs from her cigarette cartons when she babysat. Cathy and Jack are pretty young, in their early twenties. Have a three-year-old daughter named Sara.

Cathy is wearing the tightest cigarette-leg jeans. Clingy, burnt-orange scoop-neck top. Platform wedgy mules showing iridescent coral nail polish on her toes. She and Jack are going to Owen Sound. Dancing. There is a disco in one of the hotel lounges there. Something new. No band. Just recorded music. Stuff you can really dance to. Sounds good to Joan. There has not been much opportunity to dance since the Cabana burnt down.

"Yeah, you're the new lawyer's daughter, right?"

"Yes."

"You've been here with Sandy before, haven't you?"

"A couple of times."

"So you know where the booze is. Do you smoke? Help yourself. There's mix in the fridge. Do you like salt and vinegar or barbeque chips? I got both."

"Thanks."

Cathy disappears into the bathroom and comes out reeking of Babe perfume. Jack, who has been sitting in the living room, jumps up and grabs her arm, pulling her out the front door.

"Come on, let's go. They're here."

Joan goes to the front window and sees them getting into some kind of suped-up sports car with mag wheels. Cathy squeezes into the back where another woman is sitting, Jack slides in beside the guy who is driving. Wheels spin. Gravel flies. The car shoots off. Joan turns and goes back into the kitchen. Does not really feel like having booze. Grabs a coke and some chips. Starts back to the living room. Sara appears in the doorway.

"Can I have a penis butter sandwich?"

Joan has chips in her mouth. Practically chokes. "That's peanut butter," says Joan. When she can manage.

"My daddy says penis butter," insists the little girl. Joan ignores her and hunts down the peanut butter and bread. Slathers a slice. Gives it to the girl. Sara sits down at the kitchen table. "Will you read me a story after?"

"Sure," says Joan. Smiles at the kid. Might as well. Nothing on TV tonight. Only two channels available in town. From Kitchener and Wingham. Some kind of a polka show on one, not much better on the other. If you are really stoned out of your mind the polka show can be a gas. Eeeiiii Eeeiiii Oh! Lots of self-conscious farmers jumping around.

The kid has a single beat-up book in her room. *Cinderella.* Kind of cheaply illustrated. Torn, dog-eared, and grimy. Sara makes Joan read her the story at least five times. Joans keeps glancing around the room for something else to read.

"Don't you have any other books?" Joan asks.

"Only in my daddy's room. I like this one better."

"What's in your daddy's room?"

The little girl's face falls. "I'll go get them." She disappears down the hall and comes back with a stack of magazines. *Hustler, Penthouse, Playboy.*

Joan's cheeks redden. "Oh, those are just for daddy."

"Uh-uh. My daddy reads them to me," says Sara. Matter-offactly flipping through a raunchy photo spread. "When I grow up I am going to have boobs. Right now I only have pimples."

Joan kind of stutters. "Um...uh... Well, it's time for bed."

Sara scampers up onto her bed. Pulls up the covers. Snuggles down. "Sing me a song?" Joan tries to remember some children's songs. Cannot. Sings "Angie" by the Stones. One of her favourites. Sara makes her repeat it. Joan happily sings it over and over until she thinks Sara is asleep. Gathers up the dirty magazines. Creeps out of the room.

"Will you babysit me again?" Tiny voice pleading.

"Yes." Joan would like to take the little girl away with her.

Long evening. Should have brought some records or a book. Could not find anything to read except the Cinderella book and the dirty magazines. Nice stereo, but not much around to listen to. Tony Orlando and Dawn. The Captain and Tenille. Barry Manilow. Way down at the bottom of the pile of records Joan finds an album of her secret favourite performer. Freddie Fender. Could not admit this to her friends. Does not know anybody else who has one of his albums. Listens to it a few times and memorizes some songs. Pretty late. Joan stretches out on the couch. Just about to fall asleep when the front door seems almost to burst open. Jack and Cathy and their two friends kind of trip in. All of them plastered. Pretty obviously.

Jack heads straight for the liquor cabinet and starts pouring drinks. "What'll you have?" he asks Joan.

"No. It's okay. I have to get going."

"Hey, what's your hurry?" He staggers over to the chair where his friend's wife is sitting. Sticks his hand down her top. The woman tips her head back and rubs her cheek against his crotch. "Do you know Doug and Lori?"

"Um, no."

"We were just going to get some hot stuff going." Joan stares as Jack opens Lori's blouse. Unclasps her bra and exposes her large breasts. Starts rolling them in a circular motion. Lori starts panting and undulating her hips. Pushing her face into his bulging groin. Cathy has put some music on. Something with a throbbing drumbeat and a woman making groaning sounds. Dances in the middle of the floor. She pulls her top over her head, bra-less breasts flop free. Moves her hands to her crotch and grinds a couple of times. Lets her hands drag up her tummy until they get to her breasts. Cups them up high. Moves slowly toward Doug. Shoves her boobs into his face. Straddles him. He begins to pump his groin up and down under her crotch.

Joan picks up her jacket and her bag. "Um. Ahem. I better get going," she says lamely.

"Come on. Relax. Have a drink."

"No." Firmly. "I have to go. Do you have my pay?"

Jack looks pissed off. "Awright. Here." Digs his wallet out of his pocket. Throws a couple of bills at her. Joan tries to catch them as they float towards her. Ends up having to bend down to pick them up. Cheeks burning. Stuffs the money in her pocket.

"Thanks. Bye." Gets out the door as fast as she can. It's two-thirty in the morning. Cathy and Jack live in a new house on the highway on the way out of town. Joan had walked over. Expecting to get a ride back. She sighs. Starts trudging along the shoulder. Pretty long walk to her place. Kind of cold and damp like August nights can be, even after a hot day. Sound of a motorcycle coming up behind her. It's slowing down. Passes her and stops on the shoulder just ahead. Joan stops. Trying to think of what she can do if the guy tries to grab her.

"Hey, sexy mama." Joan relaxes. It's Zeke the Freak. For once she is happy to see him. "What's a nice girl like you doing in a place like this? Want a ride?"

"Yes. Please."

"Oh. So you can be nice when you want something."

"Come on, Zeke…." Impatient. "The weirdest thing just happened to me." She starts telling him about Jack and Cathy.

"Holy shit. For a little town this place has got lots of action."

"Oh, for fuck's sake, Zeke."

"Yeah, exactly."

She gets on the back of his bike and he takes her into town. Joan is tired. Lets her head rest on his back. Smells his male smell on the well worn-denim of his jacket. Arms round his waist. Feels hard muscles moving along his sides as he steers the bike. She is thinking that he does have a nice body. Such a pain in the ass most of the time, though.

They are just about at her house when Sandy jumps out onto the street and flags them down. "Been waiting for you to get home forever." Martin must have given her some speed or something. Sandy is tripping pretty heavy. Kind of shaky. Eyes wide and gleaming.

"Got something to tell you. I think I know why Martin left Linda."

"It was Linda..." Joan starts to say.

"No, no, no." Sandy cuts her off. She gets all incoherent and Joan cannot make her out.

Joan grabs her by the shoulders. "Slow down. Are you okay?" She is thinking about everything Linda told her. Weird ceremonies. Getting tied up. Getting cut up. Should have told Sandy. Even though she promised. Linda should not be keeping it quiet. Who cares about Martin's stupid law career? Joan suddenly shudders. What if Martin came back to town to be her father's partner?

Sandy is calming down. Catching her breath. "He's got this thing about virgins. Didn't stop talking about it all night. So, he and Linda did it. Then he didn't want her anymore. That's why he isn't interested in me now, either. He kind of made me tell him. It was kind of weird. He made me tell him every little detail about how I lost my virginity. He was really getting off on it. Kept questioning me and questioning me. I thought he was really into me because, you know... I'm a woman now. Then he goes, 'well you won't do'... Because he's looking for a virgin."

Joan is relieved. Let Sandy think what she wants. Does not have to worry about her getting hurt now. Does not have to worry about breaking her promise to Linda.

"So, that's why he's interested in you," says Sandy.

Zeke starts to laugh. Joan's cheeks are burning. "What makes him think that I'm a virgin?"

"Oh. Sorry."

"You told him?" Spitting angry.

Zeke is now roaring with laughter. "Glad to be of service to you, Joan. Anything else you need…just let me know." Guns his motorcycle. Heads out of town.

Joan shoves her hands into her pockets. Feels the bills Jack gave her. Pulls them out. Had not really looked at them. Just glad to get out. There is a twenty and a fifty! Fucking shit! Best babysitting money she ever made.

She stares at the money. "Here." She offers the money to Sandy.

"What's that for?"

"It's a long story." Should she tell Sandy about her cousin? Joan feels a heavy burden of small-town secrets weighing her down.

gravel run

For nearly a week Sandy has not called. Joan is hanging around with Linda a lot now, which makes Sandy too jealous. Joan does not see why it is such a problem for Sandy if she has other friends. Puts down the phone. Screw Sandy. Gets her jacket and bag and goes out to the car. Drives out to the golf course. Linda should be just getting off work.

Linda has one of the best jobs in town. Hostess in the dining room at the golf course. The pay is higher than a regular waitress, plus she gets a share in the tips that the other waitresses make. They have to be really nice to her or she does not give them good tables in their sections. She also gets to hire. Linda said Joan could have a job there after one of the girls left this summer. Joan is happy at the steak house, though.

Linda is just getting on her ten-speed as Joan pulls up. She looks tired and is happy to load her bike into the trunk of the big grey boat of a car. It's like a boat because it seems to float above the road, absorbing bumps with a rocking motion. Front and rear bench seats stretch expansively. Up to ten kids have been crammed into the old beater. Unlimited use of her mother's car has made this summer a dream for Joan. Except, of course, that Elliot went away and now Zeke the Freak will not leave her alone.

"Thanks a million for the lift. My back is killing me. Bending over those handlebars would have been murder." Linda has a ten-speed Peugeot racing bike. Joan eyes its slim, elegant lines enviously.

"I guess you probably just want to go home then."

"Yeah, maybe that would be best."

They drive along in silence. It's only about eight but the sun is already slanting acutely. Summer is waning. Labour day weekend is only a couple of weeks away. Then Linda and her whole gang, Joan's new friends, will be gone. To university. Or to college. Joan cannot wait until it is her turn to get out of this town.

"Hey, look! It's Janey and the guys." Linda points.

Linda's friends, now Joan's, are grouped around the park bench in front of the bank at the main intersection of town. Kids in town hang out there when there is nothing else to do. At some point or other on any given evening chances are anybody you might want to see will pass by the bank corner. Linda rolls down her window and calls to Janey. Joan pulls the car over. Janey comes over and leans her head in the window. The three guys hang back behind her. There is Ed, who is Janey's boyfriend. Everyone calls him Fast Eddy. Not so original, but it stuck. All through high school Linda and Martin, Janey and Ed were a team. Janey and Fast Eddy still hang around with Linda now that she and Martin have split up.

There is Jimmy Jesus, who drifted into town early in the summer. He really looks like Jesus. Long, golden-brown hair and beard. Piercing blue eyes. A really quiet guy. Everybody thinks he is deep. Linda has been getting cuddly with him ever since she stopped going out with Martin.

And there is Drew. The most sophisticated. So sarcastic. Always has a smart comeback delivered in a hilarious whiny drawl. Even though Drew is older Joan knows him from being in the drama club at school. Drew is the one who is always staging unusual projects. Always seems to find out about the latest avante-garde things before anybody else does. Always going down to Toronto to see strange dance and music happenings. People say he has a lover in Toronto. An older woman. An artist. This last school year he kept doing things he called performance art in the hallways of the school. They were always really weird and Joan never understood them, but she knew they all had some really cosmic meaning. Got him lots of coverage in the yearbook. Joan likes to be around him. Makes her feel like she is part of something bigger than all the small town shit she puts up with.

"So, what are you guys up to?" says Linda.

"Oh, we were just going to stroll over to the bistro, get some espresso, and take in a poetry reading," drawls Drew.

Linda and Joan giggle. "What's a bistro?" asks Fast Eddy.

"We don't really have any plans," says Janey.

Fast Eddy nudges Janey out of the way and sticks his head in the window. Looks into the back seat, nods approvingly. "Nice car. This would be a great car for a gravel run."

Joan tenses. She has never taken the car on a gravel run before. Has always been careful to avoid it. If her mother ever found out... But then. After all, it is probably safer if she is driving. She does not drink all that much. When she has been out on gravel runs before it has usually made her nervous watching the driver down beer after beer. So this time she can actually be in control. Okay. Why not?

"There's lots of room. Hop in." They all pile in. Linda moves to the back to be beside Jimmy Jesus. Joan ends up with Drew beside her in the front.

"Where are we going to get beer? The beer store is closed."

"No need," says Jimmy Jesus, holding up a plastic bag with some white powder in it. "Crystal THC." Jimmy is the best source in town for chemicals these days.

"Great. Let's go out to the drive-in first," says Fast Eddy.

Joan swings the car around and heads it out to the drive-in that is on the highway going out of town. They pull up to one of the picnic tables at the back. Everybody gets out and sits. Jimmy Jesus cannot find anything else so he starts to cut up lines right on the table-top. At least it is a painted picnic table. Fast Eddy goes to the drive-in window to get some Cokes. He comes back with some fries and pizza slices, too.

"You won't be getting as high if you eat," says Jimmy Jesus flatly.

"I'm starved," says Fast Eddy, with his mouth full. Joan takes some fries. Looks at the carefully apportioned lines arrayed in front of Jimmy Jesus. Two each. What if she did just one? Does not know what driving would be like high on THC.

"Who's got a bill?" asks Jimmy Jesus.

"Here," says Drew, pulling a one out of his wallet. Hands it over to Jimmy Jesus, who rolls it up tightly and starts to snort his two lines. Drew takes out another one and starts to fiddle around with it. "Did you know that if you fold it like this it looks like the Queen's..." He breaks off and shows the folded bill to the other two guys. They start to snicker.

"Let me see," says Joan. Drew shows her. She cannot figure out what she is supposed to be seeing, but she lets a knowing grin spread across her face and nods as if she can see it. Linda and Janey start to snicker, too.

"Come on. Let's get these done before they blow away," says Jimmy Jesus. One by one the others all snort up their lines. Lots of sniffing and throat clearing. Joan is handed the rolled-up bill. She moves round the table to where the last two lines are laid out. She has to stretch in front of Jimmy Jesus to get her nose over them. She sticks the bill into her right nostril. It is faintly damp from being in everybody else's noses. With a finger over her other nostril she inhales the line through the rolled bill. Large chunks of powder hit the back of her throat. Has to take a drink of Coke because of the chemical burn. Looks around the group. They are all watching expectantly. Looks like she has no choice. She goes for it.

They get back in the car. It is twilight now and a luminous sky hovers over a darkened landscape. Joan turns the car onto one of her favourite concession roads. Takes you to the highest part of the township, where you can look down over the rolling farm-land to the lake below. They get to the top just in time to see the last section of the sun sink into the lake. A few garishly orange clouds stand out against a violet sky.

"Mother Nature has questionable taste in colour sometimes," drawls Drew. Joan laughs, but she is thinking how marvelous the colours are.

"Even though I broke up with Martin, this has been a great summer," sighs Linda. "I'm glad. I'll have something to remember when I go away to university."

"You should take a year off. Come hitchhiking with me. We can see the country," says Jimmy Jesus.

Linda laughs. "Right. My parents will be happy to pay for my education after that."

Joan glances in her rear-view mirror. Jimmy is staring straight ahead. Glowering. Linda does not seem to notice.

Joan spots a road she does not think she has ever been on before and turns the car onto that. It is a narrow, low-lying road that runs through a tunnel of overhanging trees. Wherever the road dips wisps of mist have settled across it. Nosing the car through the mist, Joan feels like she is travelling back in time. There is nothing to indicate that she has not. No power lines run along this road. Old split-rail fences line either side. If they stopped at a farmhouse along the way, would they be greeted by people in turn-of-the century clothes?

Driving is like magic. Joan keeps a steady foot on the gas and anticipates every dip and turn in the road. The car sails smoothly over ruts and potholes. The sides of Joan's mouth pull outwards into a smile. She drives, eyes forward, oblivious to everything but the rapture of driving. The others feel the magic, too. Silence in the car. Six faces, lit only by the dash lights, stare straight ahead. Mona Lisa smiles on each face. The old, winding road comes to an end. Then they are on a wide, well-graded concession road. Next a short run on the highway. Turning again onto the back roads. Joan is not sure where they are. From time to time she comes to a corner she recognizes, then she loses her bearings again. Does not really matter. The roads all criss-cross. Eventually she will find herself in a familiar place. For now she just wants to keep driving.

Chug, chug, chug. The car starts to shudder. Then the engine dies. "Shit."

The others are dazed. Transition to reality has come too suddenly. "What's happenin', man?" asks Drew, doing a Cheech and Chong imitation. Everybody laughs.

"Shit," says Joan again. "I can't believe it. I ran out of gas."

They all get out of the car. Joan unfolds herself from the driver's seat. Feels like she is ten feet tall. Takes a step and has to steady herself against the car. Vertigo.

They are on an old, narrow road running alongside a river. With the car lights off, the darkness is thickly tangible. Slowly Joan's eyes start to pick shapes out of the blackness. She sees the glow of the moon on the river between the trees. All along the bank, fireflies are dancing. Stares for a while. Entranced. Starts to recognize where she is. Linda has figured it out, too.

"Your friend Zeke's place is around here, isn't it?"

"Yes," groans Joan. Zeke the Freak will never let her live this down. Joan wishes she could think of another way out, but she cannot. Starts to walk along the road towards Zeke and Draino's farmhouse. "Come on, it's this way."

The moonlight is not really bright enough to light up the road. The farmhouse is not far but the walk is not easy. Joan feels like she is towering over everybody else. Her legs are like long, rubbery pendulums swinging beneath her torso. She stumbles over and over. Drew, who is walking beside her, manages to keep her on her feet.

"Okay, everybody stop rocking the boat until Joan gets her sea legs," he calls to the others. Joan is partly embarassed, partly pleased to be the object of Drew's humour. She sees Zeke's place up ahead. Lights are on. Suddenly gets an inspiration. It could look a lot like she's with Drew tonight. The others are paired off. Then maybe Zeke would get off her case.

When they get onto the porch it is easy to see into the well-lit kitchen. Zeke and Draino are sitting at the kitchen table. Zeke is cleaning a gun and Draino is fooling around on his guitar. They are passing a joint back and forth. Before Joan can knock, Zeke the Freak and Draino look up. Six people on a wooden porch make a lot of noise. Zeke jumps up with a panicked look, then he sees Joan's face through the window. Strides over and opens the door.

"Shit, man, I thought it was the pigs or something," he says with relief. "What are you doing out here this time of night?"

Joan looks at the clock on the stove. Fuck a duck. It is 2:30 in the morning. Her mother is going to scalp her. "Um…we were out on a gravel run and I ran out of gas."

"Oh. Well, come on in and have a tea and a toke."

Joan is about to say no, but the others have already pushed past her and are sitting at the big kitchen table. Zeke the Freak fills the kettle and puts it on the stove. Joan takes a chair beside Drew. Pulls it close beside him. Draino rolls a joint and passes it around.

"Great. This is just what I need to take the edge off the THC," says Jimmy Jesus.

"You on that Crystal T that's been around?" asks Zeke.

"Yeah. Good stuff. Want to do a couple lines?"

"No, thanks."

"Joan here has been demonstrating her car's performance for us. Don't let her do any more before she gets behind the wheel again," drawls Drew. Joan giggles and gives him a slap on the shoulder. But she's puzzled. She thought her driving had been outstanding. Looks up. Sees Zeke glaring at Drew. Joan has to smile to herself.

"Well, I guess you folks will be staying the night, so you don't have to worry about that," says Zeke.

The others do not seem to mind, but Joan is terrified. "No way, I've got to get back to town."

"What do you want me to do? Take you all in one at a time on my motorcycle? Relax. Have some tea. There's lots of room here for you guys to sleep. In the morning I'll go out to the service station and bring back some gas."

"There's got to be a way. If I don't get home with the car tonight my mother will never let me drive again."

"Uh-oh. Joanie's going to be grounded," taunts Drew. Joan gives a dry laugh. Appreciating his humour less and less. Has to keep up the act for Zeke, though.

"Okay," says Zeke roughly, "I don't have any gas here. If you want gas, I'll have to siphon it out of the neighbour's car." He looks at Joan. "If I have to do that, you're going to come with me."

"Fine," says Joan weakly. The last thing she wants to do is to get up and go with Zeke. Leave the others sitting comfortably, drinking tea and toking. Got to get home, though.

"Who's the jerk you're with?" asks Zeke when they get outside.

"He's not a jerk, he's a really neat guy."

"Oh, yeah, well I'm really impressed."

She does not reply. They walk without talking. Zeke is going at a brisk pace and it is hard for her to keep up, but she is not so wrecked anymore, so at least she is not stumbling around. It is a pretty long walk to the next farm. The house is not far from the road. Not farmers here. City people who just bought a corner of land with an old stone house on it. Fixed up pretty cute. The lights are all off in the house, but the porch light is on. The car is parked over by the barn. Some kind of European car. Unfortunately the gas cap is on the side of the car that is towards the light. Zeke removes the gas cap and sticks a length of rubber tube down to the tank. Joan nervously watches the house. Imagining her parents freaking if they found out about this. Zeke sucks on the tube.

"Phaw!" He spits. "That came up real fast! I guess the tank is pretty full." He sticks the tube into the gas can he has brought. "There, that should be enough to get you back to town. Don't want to wipe these good folks out."

When they get back to the road they see headlights approaching. Zeke drops the gas can into the tall grass by the road. Grabs Joan and locks his lips onto hers. His mouth tastes like gasoline. Joan wants to retch, but she cannot break free from his grip. The car passes by. Zeke lets go. Joan spits and wipes her mouth.

Stomach heaving.

"Christ!"

"Sorry. I had to give us an alibi."

"Why don't you just give up, Zeke?"

"Hey, I am getting you and your sleazy friends out of deep shit and this is the kind of thanks I get?"

"My friends are not sleazy."

"Yeah, well, Linda's okay, but your fancy man really gets on my nerves. And Jimmy Jesus? What are you doing hanging around him? I've heard some bad things about his drugs. Don't do any more of that Crystal T."

"Who are you to tell me what I can do?"

"I'll tell you more, too. Maybe you should be paying some attention to your old friends. I'm not supposed to be telling you, but your best friend, Sandy, is in the hospital right now. She's having an abortion. Draino took her over to Owen Sound on the bike yesterday because she didn't think she could ask you to drive her."

Joan's heart drops into the pit of her stomach. She stops in her tracks. "No fucking way," she breathes. Zeke does not answer. "When does she get out?"

"Tomorrow morning."

"I am going to get her."

"Uh-uh. I promised her I wouldn't tell you."

"I don't care. I am going to get her."

Sandy is looking small and curled into herself. When she sees Joan her face lights up for a second, then she gets a pissed-off look. "Who told you?"

"Zeke the Freak."

"The motherfucker."

"Who's the father? Mr. Body Parts?"

"The motherfucker."

"Did you ever see him again?"

"The motherfucker."

Joan takes Sandy's bags and helps her down to the car. Sandy sits huddled in the front seat.

"Are you okay?" asks Joan.

"It was a nightmare in there. Do you know where they do it? In the maternity ward. All these happy expectant mothers all around me. Looking at me like 'what are you doing here?' And the nurses were horrible. But I had to do it, didn't I? There is no way I am ready for a baby."

Joan had to agree. She could not imagine Sandy coping with a baby. Sandy's mother would make her keep it, too. That would be the end of any of Sandy's hopes for the future.

"But what if I can't have one later?" Sandy almost whispers.

Joan has to go in to work after she drops Sandy off at her place. She has a late shift so she does not get to see Sandy until the next day, which is Joan's day off. They meet on the beach in the afternoon. A muggy, mid-August day. Not a breeze. Even off the lake. The waves breaking on the shore are big and choppy, though. August is the time for lake storms. It could be a fine, calm day, but the water would be angry. Somewhere out on the lake the wind is whipping up the waves. On the beach Joan and Sandy are sweltering. They have to go in for dips every half an hour. After each swim it takes no time for the sweat to be pouring off them again.

Joan is just about to get up for another dip when she sees Linda coming toward them. Linda is wearing a heavy Cowichin sweater and she is clutching it to her body as if she is cold. She sits down on their blanket and stares out at the lake, rocking her body back and forth. Shoulders hunched under the sweater.

"What's the matter, Linda?" asks Joan. Sandy sits up, too, looking concerned.

For a long time Linda does not say anything. Rocks. Stares. She is shivering. "It's so cold. I can't get warm. Have to go get a coffee." Gets up. Walks kind of aimlessly toward the tuck shop on the beach. Joan makes a move to follow her. Sandy grabs Joan's arm.

"It was Jimmy Jesus," she says. "He went over to the golf club just before Linda started work. They had a coffee at the waitress table. Jimmy put five hits of acid in Linda's coffee."

How did Sandy find out about these things? She only got out of the hospital yesterday. Joan did not think she had been out of her house until this afternoon.

"When Linda got off, she didn't know what was happening to her. She freaked out while she was working. Started throwing her tips in the garbage. All the waitresses were standing around looking at all this money in the garbage. They didn't know what to do. Then Linda just left. She didn't go home. I don't know if anybody has seen her until now."

"Well, then, let's get her home," says Joan. Just then one of the town police cars comes down onto the beach. The police chief is behind the wheel. Pulls up beside Linda. Gets out, gently takes her by the shoulders, puts her into the cruiser. Joan and Sandy watch as the car leaves the beach and makes its way up the hill toward Main Street.

shaggin wagon

Joan enters Sandy's house through the kitchen door. Without knocking. Laidie is always so pissed off when she knocks. "Come on in! Don't knock!" she calls out every time Joan comes . Takes a long time for Joan to get used to it. Even now, when Joan goes over, she wonders if she might intrude on some tense or intimate family moment and not be welcome. It has never happened. Joan cannot imagine her own mother inviting people to interrupt the privacy of their home without any warning. Sandy is able to sense this about Joan's family. She has never dared to walk in unannounced at Joan's house. Joan's mother makes all of Joan's friends call her Mrs., but Sandy's mother insists on being called 'Laidie' by everybody. Short for Adelaide. Even Sandy calls her Laidie.

Laidie is at the sink washing dishes. Her boyfriend, Chas, is sitting at the kitchen table with his chair tilted back. Picking his teeth. Looking satisfied. Sandy's youngest sister, Alison, is still pushing food around her plate. Slumped at the table with her head resting on one hand. Laidie yells "Hi!" over her shoulder. None of them even look up as Joan walks through the kitchen. Joan goes up the stairs to Sandy's room.

"They're here!" she calls ahead of herself. She has to crunch down to get through the tiny door into Sandy's room. It is in the middle of town but Sandy's house is built farm-style. The big room she and her sister Julie share is in the part of the house where the hands would bunk if it were a farm. There used to be a back stair leading down from the bunk room to the kitchen. It is boarded over and an extra washroom has been built off the kitchen where the stairwell used to be. Laidie just had this done recently. Before the divorce she and her husband shared the big bunk room. Now she has taken a smaller, cozier room in the front of the house. Joan misses the old stairway. Like a secret passage.

When Joan straightens her body on the other side of the doorway she is looking at Karen, not Sandy. "Oh," she says.

"Who's here?" asks Sandy, coming out of the walk-in closet that splits the bunk room, separating Sandy's and Julie's territories.

"Karen is here."

"Yeah." Looks at Karen and laughs. "Ha, ha, ha."

"I thought you might not know yet. Her mom and dad were at the steak house. I served them."

"Yeah, well. They are staying at our cabins."

"Hello," interrupts Karen, "stop talking as if I'm not here."

"Ha, ha, ha." Sandy's laugh rings out again. She is in a fine mood.

Karen and Joan sprawl across the bed. Toke passed around. Karen and Sandy continue what they had been doing before Joan came. Going through the closet and looking at all the clothes Sandy has gotten since the last time Karen was here. That was a year ago. Every year this ritual is repeated. Karen's family has rented the same cabin for the same two weeks every summer for as long as Sandy can remember. Sandy and Karen get along so well it always seems as if no time at all has gone by between Karen's visits.

"I'm not coming home after work tonight."

"That's quite an announcement." Joan's mother has put down

her book and is looking at Joan with a frown.

"I'm meeting Sandy and Karen at the beach and then we're going to the midnight movie."

"What's playing?"

"I don't know. Who cares? It's just for the fun of it....There isn't much else to do."

"You kids don't know how to have fun anymore. When I was your age we didn't have money to go out to movies every week. My friends and I used to have sing-songs at our house. It was fun! And we didn't need liquor or drugs. Just good, clean fun. Why don't you invite Sandy and Karen over here? We could make popcorn. It would be nice to see Sandy more often. You're always at her place. She never comes around anymore...."

Joan's mother is still talking. Joan is thinking about what she needs to take to work to get ready to go out after her shift is over. She notices silence around her. Looks up. Her mother is staring at her. Waiting for her to say something. Joan shrugs her shoulders.

"We've already got everything planned. Maybe another night, Mom."

Joan walks out of the living room and goes up to her bedroom to get her stuff together.

"You don't have any more pot?"

"No, that was the last joint last night."

Sandy stares at Karen. Unbelieving. Karen usually brings a good supply with her from the city. "Well, I don't have any," says Sandy with disdain, as if it could hardly be expected of her. They both turn to Joan.

"Don't look at me, I never have any." Joan's big concession to her parents. After all, her father is the lawyer in town. Using is one thing, possession is another.

"Shit," they all say at once.

They are at the beach, sitting on a bench facing out over the water. The sun has begun its descent to the horizon. Sky still bright, but glowing yellow. The first part of their plans for the evening were to sit there and smoke a joint. Later to battle the munchies with some fries from the beach cafe. Then to walk uptown to the midnight show. Joan has not brought the car tonight.

"Okay. So let's go for a walk on the breakwall and watch the sun go down."

"Whoopee," says Sandy, sneering.

"Go fuck yourself," says Joan.

They head morosely toward the harbour. It is the usual evening crowd. All ages. Half the people have ice creams from the beach cafe. Sauntering along, stopping to look at the yachts that have tied up for the night. People on the yachts sitting on their decks with beers, trying to ignore the sightseers. Sometimes talking to the passersby. Karen and Sandy are walking ahead. Whenever they pass a cute guy Karen's elbow jabs into Sandy's side. Giggling, heads leaning into each other. Joan is thinking about going home. It was a heavy crowd at the steak house that evening. Joan was on her feet and running for her whole shift. Karen and Sandy go back way before Joan moved to town. By now Joan and Sandy have shared more time together, but she always feels like a new friend coming between Karen and Sandy.

They turn onto the breakwall. Walking directly toward the setting sun. Everything in the foreground is black, silhouetted by dazzling sky and water. The lake is choppy and still has a bit of blue iridescence on either side of the sparkling path of light leading to the sun. Joan is thinking she does not need pot. Feels damn good to be out on the breakwall on a warm summer night. Soft breeze on her face. Incredible sunset spread out for her.

Three dark figures loom ahead. Coming toward them. Sandy and Karen are in the middle of a particularly silly fit of giggling. The figures pass by unnoticed by the two of them. Almost unnoticed by Joan, who is still wrapped up in the sunset. Something makes her turn as she comes abreast. Three guys. Joan is looking directly into the eyes of a guy whose face is half-lit by the sun behind him. Their eyes lock, but they keep on walking. Then all three guys stop and turn back, facing Joan. She stops and turns around. Joan is aware that behind her Sandy and Karen have also stopped and turned to face the guys.

Three guys caught in the blaze of the setting sun. Look to be in their early twenties. The one who snagged Joan's gaze is tall and lank, with a long, narrow nose and metal-rimmed glasses. Beside him is a well-built guy with a mustache and intense eyes. The third is kind of baby-faced. All three have longish, shaggy hair with bangs. They are all really cute. For a few seconds the two groups just stand and stare at each other. Then the tall guy smiles.

"Wanta skip soom stunes, loovs?"

Some kind of British accent. Joan is trying to place it.

"Sure," she says. Sandy and Karen need no convincing either.

The sun is completely set and they cannot skip stones anymore. Not where they are on the beach. Good distance from the harbour and away from the lights that beam down there all night. Joan can see the lights but they are far enough away that they do not really light up the shore where all of them are now sitting. This part of the beach is covered with fist-size, softly-rounded stones. In front of them the water stretches out black and blends into the sky. Behind them is Cedar Park, a nicely maintained picnic area nestled under a cedar grove. Too dark to skip stones. The guys suggest playing hide-and-seek in the dusky light among the cedars. Joan thinks, "Oh, sure." Imagines all the groping that is going to happen. Karen and Sandy readily agree. Joan sees no way but to go along with it. Turns out to be a lot of fun. Lots of shrieking and bumping into people and trees. Joan is surprised that, although she is grabbed and tackled a couple of times, no hands find their way to forbidden places. Does not take long before they are all out of breath. Getting too dark between the trees to keep playing.

They stumble out from under the cedars and collapse at a pic-nic table that has been pulled down onto the beach. For a while they sit and catch their breath, every so often breaking into giddy laughter. Joan cannot believe she had so much fun playing a kids' game.

"You guys got any tokes?" asks Sandy. Joan has not even thought about getting high since they met the guys. Sandy has got pot on her brain.

"Neva tooch tha stooff," replies the tall guy. He is the ring-leader. So far, everything has been started by him and the other two guys just follow along.

"It's a Liverpool accent!" says Joan. At last it has come to her. "You sound just like the Beatles."

"Tha's right. Gude ea-ur!"

"Hey, and you guys are just like the Beatles," says Sandy. She points to the tall guy. "You're John." She looks at the dark guy. "You're George," she says. "And you're Paul," she designates the baby-faced one. "Where's Ringo?"

"He coodn't mak it t'nat."

After that she and Karen keep calling them by Beatle names. The guys do not seem to mind. Joan realizes they have not yet told them their real names, so she starts calling them Beatle names, too. They sit and stare out into the blackness of the lake and talk for a while. The guys are full of questions about Joan's, Sandy's, and Karen's lives. Interesting questions. About what they think and feel. Not just what grade they are in and what TV shows they like, or that kind of stuff. Joan thinks these guys are really different. For one thing, not one of them has put a move on any of the girls yet.

"Wha's next, loovs?" asks John.

Joan holds her watch up so that it can catch the harbour lights. "We were going to go to the midnight movie."

"Can we join ya?"

"Sure, but it's all the way up town, so we better get going 'cause it's going to start soon."

"Not a prooblem, we c'n tek oor van."

They have to walk back to the harbour, where the van is parked. Joan does not hesitate to get in. In the back of her mind she hears her mother warning her about getting into cars with strange men, but she feels no danger with the Liverpool guys. The Beatles. Only two bucket seats in the front of the van. John drives and Joan sits in the passenger seat. Sandy, Karen, George, and Paul all sit cross-legged in the open space in the back. It is well-padded with sleeping bags, pillows, and duffel bags. Driving uptown, John takes a few corners pretty close. To make everybody in the back roll into each other. It is fun. Joan wishes she had sat in the back, but she thinks it is too late now to move. By the time they pull into the theatre parking lot they are all splitting their sides with laughter.

The parking lot is empty. The theatre is dark. Joan opens the door and gets out. She goes over to the box office. Looking for any clue. There have been midnight shows every weekend for the past month. She and Sandy just assumed there would be one this weekend. John has gotten out of the van and is standing beside her.

"Shit," she mutters, "I'm sorry."

"No worry," says John. "A'm soorta hoongry, c'n we fand a place ta get soomthin'?

"We could go to the drive-in."

At the drive-in they have a real pig-out. Even without tokes to give them the munchies, they have worked up a good appetite after all of the fun they had this evening. The girls each have a large fries and a milkshake. When they finish those, they go back and get popcorn and Cokes. The guys insist on paying for everything. They themselves have a couple of hamburgers each. And fries, milkshakes, chocolate bars, popcorn, and pop. Eat steadily for an hour. Talking and joking. All of them sitting in the back of the van. In a circle. Then the guys bring out their guitars.

They play only Beatles songs. They know the words and music to every one. Joan keeps trying to think of obscure Beatles tunes that not everyone knows. Cannot come up with a title that they are unable to play. The girls sing along wherever they can. Joan knows more lyrics than either Sandy or Karen. John beams at her when she is able to remember all of the verses of a song. Most of the time Sandy and Karen can only sing the choruses. Joan is having a great time. She loves to sing, but she usually feels self-conscious doing it in front of other people. These guys make her feel at ease. John tells her she has a great voice. She even sings one song all by herself and all the guys clap when she is finished. Karen and Sandy roll their eyes.

Joan thinks about her mother. She would be so happy to see what a fun time Joan is having tonight. No booze. No pot. The guys are real gentlemen. Even by now not one of them has so much as tried to kiss any of the girls. Exactly what her mother calls "good, clean fun." The lights in the drive-in go out. The two servers close the shutters and leave together in the same car. Parking lot is empty except for their van. The midnight movie is usually a double bill, ending around three in the morning. The girls figure they have another hour before they have to be home, since their parents think they are at the movie. They do not want the night to end.

"Did you ever meet the Beatles?" asks Joan.

"Whot? Us?"

Joan realizes it is a stupid question. Liverpool is probably a very big city. Still, she has heard that the Beatles do go back and hang out with people there. "Oh, I just thought that maybe you had got to meet them somewhere in Liverpool...." She lets the sentence trail off.

"Neva bin ta Livapool," says George flatly.

"Maybe soom dah," says John longingly.

"Waddya mean?" cries Joan.

"We're froom Kingston," says John. "We joost luv tha Bea'les."

"Yeah, so we started talking lak 'em. Been doin' it so loong, we cawn't stoop it naw," says George.

It is kind of infectious. Within a few minutes all three girls are trying on the Liverpool accent. They cannot stop either. A lot of things come out sounding pretty funny. Once again they find themselves rolling around laughing their guts out. Three o'clock comes too soon. Throughout the night there has been no pairing up of girls and guys. As they pull out of the drive-in parking lot couples form in an almost organic way. No words are spoken but each guy gravitates toward one of the girls. Joan ends up in the front with John again. Some spark between the two of them started the whole evening off. John stretches his hand between the bucket seats and takes Joan's hand. Sandy cuddles up with George, and Karen is leaning against Paul. Somehow the guys have each chosen the girl who would have chosen them if there had been any conscious thought put into it.

They get to Joan's house first. Everybody is talking about getting together the next day. Arrangements have not been finalized yet.

"You guys figure out what you want to do and give me a call," she says to Sandy and Karen. John has gotten out of the van and is holding the door open for her to get out. She steps down onto the sidewalk into his arms. He wraps her up in them, close to his chest. She breathes in his odour and it goes right to her head. He lifts her chin and gives her a warm, firm kiss on the lips. No tongue. No groping. Just sweet.

"See ya toomoorah," says John.

"Get in the house right now!" says Joan's mother. She is standing like a statue on the front porch. Cold and stony, her mouth set grimly. Either she has been standing there all along, or she managed to slip out unnoticed while Joan and John were kissing. The vision of her standing there with her arms crossed is like something out of a horror movie. John visibly jumps away from Joan and dashes around the van to get in the driver seat. Joan looks pleadingly at her mother, then turns to see the van pulling away. Pale faces of Karen and Sandy staring back at her.

"I said get in the house!" Her mother's voice cuts like a knife.

"You lied to me!" screams her mother when they are inside. "You said there was a midnight movie. I thought it would be nice if I came and picked you girls up since you didn't take the car. But I got there and found out there was no show. All along you were planning this little escapade with those tourist boys in their shaggin' wagon, weren't you?"

"It didn't happen that way…" Joan starts to explain, but her mother cuts her off.

"I don't want to hear about it. Get up to your room right now! You are grounded for the rest of the week!"

The next day Sandy phones Joan. Still talking with a Liverpool accent. Everything is fine with her and Karen. Laidie was fast asleep when they got back to Sandy's. Karen had been planning to sleep over at Sandy's, so her parents were not waiting up. Sandy thinks it is a drag that Joan cannot come with Karen and her to meet the Beatle guys at the beach cafe.

It is not very long after that when Sandy phones again. The Liverpool accent is gone. The guys showed up as promised. John was super bummed out that Joan was not able to be there, too. He was kind of surprised that Joan is still young enough to be grounded. All the guys had thought Joan, Sandy, and Karen were older. They sat and had some Cokes at the beach cafe. For about a half an hour. Then John said he was going back to Kingston. It was his van, so the other two had no choice but to go with them.

"No way!" moans Joan. She realizes that while she was with John, she had not thought of Elliot once.

"It's all your mother's fault," moans Sandy.

Joan is thinking that there might be a good reason to start seeing Zeke the Freak.

last blast of
summer

Labour Day Weekend. A bittersweet time. Starts off with a big party. Called "Carnivale." Joan's mother sniffs at this "affectation," as she calls it. It is not the right time of the year, she says, and it is not Rio de Janeiro. Yeah, yeah, thinks Joan. It is a party. Parking lot at the beach is taken over by rides and midway games. Bake sales, bingo, arts and crafts. Streets filled with tourists and townspeople milling around. All this takes place during the day on Saturday and Sunday. Saturday night is a street dance. Main intersection of town closed right off. Live band. Joan thinks it is really cool to dance out on the street with the traffic lights still switching colours overhead. Sunday night the Chamber of Commerce throws what they call a "GIANT CHICKEN BARBEQUE." Joan has this image of huge chickens standing around oversized barbeques. All of this stuff is supposed to be a final milking of the tourist dollar for the summer, but the local people enjoy the activities, too. Late Monday morning the cars start to stream out of town. By the evening it is like a ghost town. That is the bitter part. The next day it is back to school.

Saturday is a washout for Joan. She has to work a split shift. Lunch. Then a couple of hours off. Back in for dinner. Joan decides she will just sleep between shifts. Instead of checking out the midway. That way she can be rested to go to the street dance when she is finished the dinner shift. Going to be a busy night at the steak house for sure. Joan is looking forward to a pocket stuffed with tips. This is the last weekend Karen's family will be at Laidie's cabins. Karen and Sandy are doing the midway and rides. Joan will be meeting them at the dance.

Dinner shift is murder. Joan is given the section with the most tables. Lineup out the door, no time to clear tables before people claim them. Lots of big tables. From 5:30 to 9:30 Joan does not have a chance to sit down. Cannot figure out why Steve has given her the biggest section. She is the only waitress not old enough to serve drinks. Has to wait for the bartender to take the drinks to the table. Slows everything down. Cannot complain at the end of the shift. Cashes in her tips for bigger bills and ends up with a good-sized wad. Usually she makes more in tips than she does in pay working a dinner hour. Tonight, she thinks she has had the best haul of the summer.

Joan has a Coke and a cigarette. She had been tired but now feels the energy seeping back into her. Goes down to the staff washroom and gets her street clothes out of her locker. Pretty much all the other waitresses are going to the street dance. Too crowded to get near the mirror. A cloud of hairspray and perfume makes breathing difficult. Joan struggles into a black dance leotard. It is the only thing she has been able to find that gives her a smooth body-fit . Has a graceful neckline that she thinks is elegant. Shopping in the area is the shits. With the leotard she has chosen to wear a crinkle-cotton skirt and water-buffalo sandals with toe straps both of which she got in an Indian shop the last time she was in Toronto.

"Paki clothes!" screams one of the waitresses, a particularly coarse farm girl named Erin, who Joan does not like. Joan sighs. She does not care. She loves the way the skirt moves and brushes against her bare legs. Likes the barefoot feeling of the sandals, which have just a couple of straps keeping the smooth leather soles on her feet. Nice and slippy for dancing. Erin has been hogging the mirror for about ten minutes now. Joan thinks Erin could primp there all night long and it would not help.

"Ever met a Paki?" Joan asks, evenly.

"No, but..." She is about to go on, but Joan cuts her off.

"Then shut the fuck up about it and let somebody else use the mirror."

Erin moves away and Joan stands in front of the mirror to brush her hair. Tonight her hair is cooperating. Falling to her shoulders in soft waves. She wishes it did not smell like deep-fried foods, but there is no time to wash her hair. Already 10:30 and the dance is probably in full swing. Joan is pleased with the way she looks and decides not to put on the eyeshadow she has brought along. She throws her bag over her shoulder and breezes out of the washroom, leaving the rest of the waitresses grooming and giggling.

As Joan steps out the door of the steak house the bass notes of the band throb deeply against her body. She looks down the street toward the main intersection. There is a huge crowd of people. Hundreds of heads bobbing around the band platform, which is lit up with coloured lights and strobes. The dance started at 9:00. Joan knows that for the first hour the band would have played slower songs for the oldsters. Now they are heating things up with rock tunes. In a little while the old people will drift away, leaving only kids and adults who are young at heart.

Joan breaks into a trot. The music and excitement have added to her energy. When she gets to the intersection she skirts the perimeter of the crowd. Looking for Sandy and Karen, but she does not see them. People are packed so tightly that she cannot find a place to enter the crush. Walks on tip-toes, looking for anybody she can recognize. Joan glances over her shoulder and sees Zeke the Freak coming down the street toward her. Pretending not to see him she pushes rudely into the crowd. A few dirty looks, but she manages to penetrate well toward the centre. Looking back she sees Zeke the Freak craning his neck to see into the crowd. Joan slouches low so he will not notice her. Turns to find herself face to face with Martin, the minister's son.

Being with Zeke the Freak does not seem like such a bad thing now. Joan pans the crowd with her eyes but he has disappeared from view. Catches a glimpse of Drew. If she is dancing with Drew, the minister's son will keep his distance, she thinks. Besides, the band is playing a great song and Drew is a fantastic dancer. Joan gives Martin a quick smile, and before he can say anything she starts plowing her way toward Drew.

"Hey, Drew! Wanna dance?" she calls. He does not seem to have heard her. Does not turn toward her. Stands with arms crossed, watching the band. She gets closer, yells louder. "C'mon and dance!"

Drew turns toward her with a tight, little smile and shakes his head slightly. His lips mouth the word "No" silently. Joan grabs his arm and pulls. "I really want to dance," she pleads. Drew resists, giving her an icy glare. Joan sways her body to the music. Smiling, still trying to pull him toward the dance floor. He shakes her off.

"What makes you think I would want to dance with a little hick-town lawyer's daughter?" he hisses. "What makes you think I'm interested in girls at all? Have you ever seen me with a girlfriend? Haven't you figured out that I'm a faggot? I've got a fabulous lover in the city and I don't need any small-town cunts!"

Joan stands speechless for a minute. Her stomach balls up into a knot. She should not have tried to make Zeke the Freak think Drew was her boyfriend when they got stranded at his place. Always thought Drew was neat and fun to be with. Deep down maybe she knew he was homo. Never thought of him as a guy to go out with, even though she thought he was cool. Drew had obviously gotten the wrong message from her.

"Christ! All I wanted to do was dance, not fuck you!" She sneers back at him.

Then the minister's son is there. Shit. She forgot that Martin and Drew are hanging out together again now that Linda is in the loony bin.

"Joan doesn't fuck anyone. Right, little virgin?" he says teasingly.

Joan sees Sandy's head bobbing up and down in the centre of the dance crowd. Dancing with Draino. "I gotta go," she says, "I'm supposed to meet Sandy."

"Oh, that's right," says Martin, "you're best friends with that little whore."

Joan throws him a disgusted look and dives between the people. A fight to get to the centre of the mob of dancers. When she gets there Sandy is nowhere to be found. Joan glances up at the band. Cringes a bit. It is the band that she screwed up with. The guys she insulted, ruining a chance for Sandy and her to have boyfriends in a band. Whenever Sandy thinks about it she still gets upset. Joan decides maybe it would be better to give Sandy a little space tonight. She moves off toward the edge of the dance crowd. Turns to watch the band and see if she can see anybody else she knows.

Ends up standing beside a really hunky guy. Longish, straight blonde hair. Neatly cut. Tall, well-built. Sort of European-looking, Joan thinks, but she cannot say why. Dressed all in black. Nicely fitting long-sleeved T-shirt. Cigarette-legged jeans tucked into high leather boots. He leans over close to her ear and says "Hello" almost in a whisper. She looks into his eyes. They are a piercing grey-blue under perfectly regular brows. His face is like a drawing of Prince Charming from one of her childhood fairy-tale books. She cannot think of any guy she has ever met, not even that she has seen in the movies, who is more handsome. So awestruck that she can barely croak out a hello in return.

"Are you from around here?" he asks.

"No," she lies. A guy like this would never be interested in some local yokel. "Um, I'm from Toronto." Thinks she knows Toronto well enough that she can blunder her way, if asked. But he does not question her any further.

"Do you want to go for a walk?"

"Don't you want to dance?" asks Joan. Does not want to leave. Wants people to see her dancing with this guy. "I just got here, and I really want to dance."

"Maybe when the dance is over we could walk down to the beach or something."

"Sure," says Joan, "that'd be nice." She turns to look at the band and starts swaying to the music, to show him how much she wants to dance. When she looks back at him, he is gone. Weird. Hopes she will be able to find him again at the end of the dance. Joan sees Sandy again. Standing on the other side of the dance crowd with Karen and Draino. Joan really wants to dance. The music is good and there have not been any dances since the Cabana burned down. If she is with Sandy and the others, she could be dancing. Even if she ends up dancing with Zeke the Freak, it would be alright.

Joan decides the fastest way to get to Sandy, Karen, and Draino would be to go around the edge of the crowd. She forces her way out and is able to walk easily around to the other side. Tries to squeeze back through the people to get to where Sandy, Karen, and Draino are. The band is playing a really popular tune now and lots of people are rushing toward the centre to dance. Joan is caught up in the movement and swept inward. She looks around her but cannot see Sandy, Karen, or Draino. Starts dancing just by herself, but is feeling kind of foolish. After she has been drinking or toking she does not mind dancing by herself. Perfectly straight she feels awkward doing it. That is another thing, she thinks. Not even had a toke yet tonight.

"Hey, Paki-lover!" she hears. Looks around to see Erin and her friends. Good enough reason to move on. Makes her way to the edge of the crowd.

"I understand you're a Paki-lover," comes a voice from behind her. "An admirable quality."

Joan swings around to find an older man smiling at her. Very distinguished looking, but cool. Neatly groomed goatee and mustache. Layered salt and pepper hair covering the tops of his ears and brushing his turtleneck collar. Tweedy kind of jacket and blue jeans. If he had a beret on his head Joan thinks he would look just like a movie director. Artsy and interesting. Joan smiles, but she is not sure what to say.

"How did you come to have such a fine reputation?" continued the man.

"Oh, they're just a bunch of jerks who should keep their mouths shut because every time they open them something stupid comes out," says Joan, motioning with her head toward Erin's group.

"I think you're right there. It's not often you see such wisdom in a girl of your age."

Joan is beginning to feel smug. Such a sophisticated and cultured man. Finally someone who is able to see that she is different.

"Do you live around here?" he asks.

"No, um, my family is renting a cottage here and they dragged me along. What a bore." She finds herself lying again.

"I'd really like to get to know you better. Why don't we find someplace quiet where we can get a coffee and talk."

Sounds fine to Joan. She can imagine herself having a long, deep conversation with this man. Talking about books and art. The kind of talk she never gets to have with anybody in this town. Cannot think of a place to go, though. It is now midnight and pretty much everything is closed as far as coffee shops go. There is the drive-in, but it does not seem a dignified enough place to suggest. Now she can see where Drew's snide little jokes about "bistros" came from. The best thing to do is to stay here, she thinks. There is another hour for the dance to go, too, and she has not really had a dance yet.

"Wouldn't you like to dance a bit, first?" she asks.

The man looks at her oddly. "Not really," he replies. Looking at him Joan realizes she cannot really picture him dancing. There is an awkward pause. The man kind of shuffles sideways around her and excuses himself. For some reason Joan gets shivers down her spine. Shrugs it off and continues her search for Sandy, Karen, and Draino. Even Zeke the Freak. That is when she sees this tall guy with a badly scarred, caved-in face. Vaguely familiar. He turns toward her and smiles. When she sees the other side of his face she realizes who it is. B.J.! Cannot believe her eyes. How many times this summer have people turned up that she thought were dead? Looks like he nearly was. The left side of his head is hardly recognizable.

He rushes over and gives her a big hug. Shaking like a leaf. Voice all creaky. "Joan, am I glad to see you!"

"Wow, B.J. What a surprise!" is all she can think of to say.

"I'm tryna find Barb. Do you know where Barb is?"

Joan's head spins. Wonders if she should tell him. Remembers the hunted look in Barb/Brandy's eyes, telling the story of her ordeal with the bike gangs. "Are you still with a gang?" she asks.

"No, no, it's alright, Joan," he says with urgency. "It's gonna be okay. I gotta find Barb. She's the only one for me...." His voice trails off.

Joan thinks he is sincere. She tells him the whole story of their meeting GI Joe. "You can probably find her somewhere around the military base," she says. B.J. takes off without saying good-bye. A driven man, she thinks.

"Are you ready to go for that walk?" comes a whisper in her ear. Prince Charming has appeared beside her.

Suddenly she is offended by this. "You won't even dance with me," she says through clenched teeth. "I hardly even know you and you want me to go off to some secluded place alone with you?" He backs away. Joan continues plowing through the crowd. On a mission now. Only forty-five minutes left of the dance. Wants to get high. Wants to dance. Wants to be with friends. Cannot see anybody she knows. She does see Prince Charming and the movie director standing together talking. Funny, she thinks.

Drew is coming toward her. Looks behind to see if the minister's son is with him. Not there. Joan breathes a sigh of relief. "Hey, uh, sorry about what I said earlier," Drew tells her.

"S'okay," she says warily.

"Saw you talking with the new guy in town."

"New guy?" Prince Charming lives here?

"Yeah, they moved in on our street. He looks really interesting. His father's the new art teacher at the high school. What's he like?"

"Oh, I dunno." She looks across the dance crowd. Prince Charming and the movie director are still talking. "Who's that guy he's talking with now?"

"That's the new art teacher."

Things are getting too weird. Come on to by a father and his son on the same night. Joan needs to sit down. Squeezes herself out of the crowd. Quite a few people are sitting on the street curbs. No other place to sit. Joan finds a spot away from most of the other people and sinks down. That is where Sandy, Karen, Draino, and Zeke the Freak find her.

"We've been looking for you all night!"

"I've been here," Joan answers with a weary voice.

Zeke the Freak whips out a joint. Lights it. Hands it to Joan.

"You get the first toke," he says. "Take a few, you look like you need it." Joan gratefully accepts.

"This is the guy you've been trying to avoid all summer?" whispers Karen in her ear. Joan has given Karen the full rundown about Zeke the Freak. "I think he's really nice—and cute."

Well, maybe. Joan looks at Zeke the Freak. Or maybe not. She is starting to get really high and is not sure of her judgement.

Sandy laughs. "Can you believe it's the band?"

"Yeah," breathes Joan. "Sorry."

Sandy just smirks. Joan sees that Draino has his arm around Sandy's waist. Tightly. Sandy looks into Draino's eyes and smiles. Half an hour left to dance. The whole group joins the dance crowd. Stoned. Dancing. Ecstasy. Joan's mind leaves her body and floats above the group. Still attached by that silver thread. High above the dance crowd now. On the sidelines she can see the minister's son, Drew, Prince Charming, and the movie director. They are all watching her.

The chicken barbeque is set up on the beach. An area secured by a snow-fence barrier. It is completely packed. Joan is glad she and Zeke the Freak got here early and saved a table. Sitting with him for forty-five minutes, waiting for the others, was kind of nice. They had a couple of doobs and he sneaked her a beer in a plastic pop cup. Nice long chat. Zeke the Freak is actually pretty smart and has done a lot of reading. When Sandy, Karen, and Draino get there, he and Draino insist that the girls stay seated while they stand in line for the food. Dying of the munchies after the tokes she had. The guys bring back plates piled high with chicken, baked potatoes, salad and buns. Intense eating of the seriously stoned. After a while they all come up for air. Cigarettes lit. More smuggled beer poured. Joan sits back and scans the crowd.

Over in one corner Martin, the minister's son, Drew, and a bunch of other grade thirteeners from last year are having a final bash. Most of them heading off to university tomorrow. Not Linda, thinks Joan sadly. Joan has heard that the minister's son is going to Queen's. Pretty far away. Should not be back very often. Joan smiles. Drew will be at U of T. Happy with his lover. Joan wonders how many other people in town know Drew's secret.

At the entrance to the barbeque area she sees Prince Charming and the movie director on their way out. Between them walks a girl who looks to be about fifteen years old. Not from around here. Joan does not recognize her. A young, pretty tourist girl whose parents have given her some freedom for the evening. Joan sees the father-son thing that happened last night was not a coincidence. First day of school is going to be interesting. Joan is planning to take art.

Just as they are thinking about leaving, B.J. and Barb/Brandy appear and squeeze in at their table. For a minute Sandy does not recognize B.J. because of his scars. Then she lets out a screech. Joan forgot to tell Sandy she had seen B.J. last night.

"You found her!" Joan congratulates B.J. He beams. Barb/Brandy beams, too. "What happened to GI Joe?" Joan asks Barb/Brandy.

"History. I've got B.J. back." She snuggles up to B.J.

"So, Brandy," says Sandy, "I thought you couldn't be seen around here."

"You can call me Barb. I've decided it's Barb, again."

"Don't worry, I'm gonna take care of her," says B.J. "Besides, we're gettin' out. Just stopped by t' say g'bye."

Barb has been struggling with her food. Eating with her left hand only. Finally she has to give up. The hand that has been wedged in between her and B.J. comes up to stabilize the chicken breast she is trying to eat. Like a claw. Two fingers missing. Ring finger and pinky. Seems to be little movement left in the rest of the hand. Barb looks up and sees everybody is looking.

"Car accident," she says. "Well, you saw how he drove," she says to Joan and Sandy. Pause. Barb gets an eerie and disturbed look on her face. "He was kind of crazy." In a low, quavering voice. Joan guesses she is talking about GI Joe.

"Easy now," says B.J. "I'm taking you away now. Everything is gonna be okay." Barb collapses into his lap, sobbing. B.J. holds her tight. The table is silent. B.J. helps her stand up and leads her away. Joan and Sandy get up and follow after him to give her a hug good-bye. They watch him guide her out of the barbeque area and seat her on the back of his bike. After B.J. and Barb have disappeared up the hill Joan and Sandy turn around to see Karen, Draino, and Zeke the Freak staring at them with puzzled looks. Joan realizes none of them know who B.J. and Barb are.

"It's a long story" says Sandy. "Better have another toke."

Monday. Labour Day. Joan goes over to the bank corner in the afternoon. Maybe eight or nine kids there. Sitting on the bench out front or on the stairs, slouching against the wall of the bank. Watching the traffic. Family-filled cars, loaded with luggage. Bumper to bumper, hour after hour. Funnelling out of town and down from all the other resort towns to the north. After a while Joan gets tired of watching. Decides to walk down to the beach. Down through the cottages. All neatly nailed shut with boards painted matching colours. Patio lanterns taken down, lawn furniture taken in, cars gone from every driveway. By the lake a brisk wind is whipping up the sand. Not a summer breeze. Chilly. Joan hunches her shoulders and tucks her hands under her arms. The beach is deserted. Beach cafe closed and boarded up.

Joan walks out to the end of the breakwall. Sits with her legs dangling over the edge. Stares out at the horizon. Sky no longer the deep blue of summer, but cool and pale. The lake is choppy and steely grey. The wind has lifted spiky waves on the water's surface that lap at the soles of her shoes from time to time. Joan does not notice Zeke the Freak has come up behind until he sits down beside her. She smiles. He nods and pulls out a joint. They share some tokes. They sit for a long time without talking. Watching the lake.

good people

First day of school. Big fuss over the new guy. Prince Charming. Not too many new faces in this town. Same people year in and year out. Prince Charming is particularly intriguing. Really cute and such neat clothes. Kind of mysterious. Everybody wants to know about him. Somehow they all know that Joan had talked to him at the street dance. Of course, it is inevitable that she crosses Prince Charming's path at some point. The school is just not that big. He stops right in front of her, sort of looming over her.

"I thought you were not from around here."

"Well, not originally," she answers, cringing at the tone of accusation in his voice.

"But you live here, not in Toronto."

"Um…yeah."

"So, why'd you tell me you were from Toronto?"

Her face reddens. "Sorry, I thought you were a tourist."

He takes off down the hall. A group of girls surrounds her immediately.

"Wow, how did you get to know him?" "What's his name?" "Are you going out with him?"

Joan thinks about leading them on. Making them think she is dating him. Decides against it. Just shrugs her shoulders and heads toward her next class.

✦

Got through the week okay in spite of weird feelings from the new art teacher and Prince Charming. Sandy is working all weekend, helping Laidie clean out and close up the cottages. It is Saturday and Joan is working ten to two. Zeke the Freak drops into the coffee shop a little after ten. The place is not busy. Joan lights up a cigarette. Stands across the counter and chats while he has coffee and toast.

"Why don't I come by and pick you up after work?"

Joan blows a few smoke rings before she answers. "Okay."

"Great. I've got something I want to show you out at my place."

Joan is light on her feet the rest of her shift. Finds herself humming along to the Neil Diamond eight-track that plays endlessly over the dining room sound system. Most of the time she feels like ripping the tape out of the player and tossing it in the deep fryer. Today she is dreamily singing the words to songs she detests. She is happy, she realizes. Looking forward to seeing Zeke the Freak after work.

At two on the dot she looks out the front door and sees Zeke sitting on his bike, waiting. Joan runs down to the staff washroom to get changed. Nearly knocks over Steve as she bolts out the door. Outside the steak house she runs smack into Prince Charming.

"Oof. Sorry." Looks over her shoulder with an apologetic expression, but does not stop. Climbs on the bike behind Zeke. He guns the engine and shoots off from the curb. Joan glances back and sees Prince Charming staring at her with a stunned look on his face.

Soon they are on the winding road to Zeke the Freak's place. The first full weekend of September. Still warm and summery but the trees are beginning to show colours in patches here and there. Monarch butterflies hang in the air. This time of year there are hundreds of them. On the bike they have to duck now and then so they will not get hit in the face. They follow the sparkling river, brilliant in the sunlight and reflecting a jewel-blue sky. Along the other side of the road cornfields are still standing. They will have to be cut down soon. Corn is over now.

The farmhouse kitchen is cheery and inviting. Joan has not been there very often in the daytime. Sun slanting in through the windows. Joan notices for the first time that from the house's high point on the land there is a broad vista of farmland, cut through by the river, visible through windows on all sides of the house. Unlike other guys that Joan knows who are living on their own, Zeke the Freak and Draino have made their place comfortable and cozy.

Zeke the Freak steps in behind her and closes the kitchen door. He whistles and Joan hears a rustling and a clicking of paws on the floor upstairs. Pounding down the stairs. A sleek, young hound appears at the kitchen door. The hound's body begins to wriggle and shake as soon as he sees Zeke the Freak. Zeke the Freak slaps his hands on his thighs and the hound puts his front paws against Zeke's legs. The hound's tail whips at Joan as she tries to pet the dog. She stands back.

"This is Ranger," Zeke introduces the dog. "Purebred blue-tick. Aren't ya, Aren't ya," he says, using a baby-talk voice for the dog. "Got him from a farmer down the road."

"Sure is a beauty," says Joan, still not sure how to approach the hound without getting a lashing.

Zeke settles the dog down to the floor and sits down beside him. Joan kneels and fondles Ranger behind the ears.

"Want to go for a walk?" Zeke the Freak asks Joan. Before she can answer, the dog lets out a strangled bark as if to say yes, but not too enthusiastically in case of disappointment. They both laugh. "He hasn't had much training, but I think he's still young enough. I thought we could go out today and get started."

Joan thinks a nice walk on a beautiful day with Zeke the Freak and his new dog sounds good. They set off across the field, heading for the woods in the low-lying land by the river. Walking across the field is fine. Ranger runs circles around them, burning off energy from being in the house all day. Zeke the Freak does not seem to be making much effort to train the dog. They enter the woods and follow a path along the river for a while. Ranger disappears into the bush from time to time. They can hear him crashing through the underbrush, then breaking out onto the path unexpectedly. They come to a fork in the path and Zeke the Freak chooses a direction that leads them away from the river. In a few minutes the path is petering out and Joan finds herself fighting branches to make her way. The ground has become marshy. Joan is wearing sneakers and her feet are getting soggy and uncomfortable. The sun does not penetrate the dense bush, and the waterlogged soil is quite cold.

"Can't we go back to the other path?" Joan moans.

"More likely to come across a coon in this part of the woods."

"So?"

"Well...remember? I'm trying to train Ranger."

Joan looks dumbly at Zeke the Freak.

"I need a good hunting dog."

Joan thinks back to the spring. The big pig roast where she got so high on peyote. All the guns locked up in the rack upstairs in the hall. She had not even thought about it since then. Why else would he have the guns? A hunter. Joan is not so sure she is comfortable with Zeke the Freak being a hunter.

"So, what're we supposed to be doing to train Ranger?" she asks.

"He's got to get the scent."

"Well, we've been out here for a while, he musta smelled something by now...." Joan ventures hopefully.

"He'll let us know when he finds something."

"Uh-huh?" Joan is starting to get suspicious.

"Oh, yeah, he'll be baying away once he trees it."

"Then we can go after that?"

"Well...gotta get it down so he can go at it."

"Whaddya mean?"

"Um. The first couple of times you got to let them tear it up and get a taste for it...."

"No fucking way!" Joan interrupts. She glares at Zeke the Freak. "Jesus Fucking Christ!" she yells. "How could you think I would want to watch something like that?" She is shaking with anger.

"Okay, okay. Calm down."

"You are such an asshole!" she explodes. "Even if it weren't for that, this is no fun. I'm stumbling around in the bush, my jeans are soaked up to the knees—this isn't a walk , it's torture."

"Okay, I'm sorry. We can go back to my place. You can warm up and dry off." He thinks for a minute. "No, wait. I'll take you someplace even better. You're gonna love it."

Joan is angry. She would like to storm off and just leave Zeke the Freak standing there, but she does not really know where she is. No choice except to follow behind Zeke the Freak, pushing their way through the bush. Probably fifteen more minutes before they break out on the other side of the wood. Feels like hours to Joan. She mutters and swears as she tries to keep from being thrashed by the underbrush. Ranger keeps rushing out of the bush and happily jumping up on her.

"Wow, he's really getting to like you."

Joan scowls at Zeke the Freak. Her heart feels like a searing, white-hot stone.

They clear the woods. Standing at the edge of a large field. The land humps up from the the woods quite steeply. In spite of the climb ahead, Joan is relieved to be free of the bush. She takes a step forward and feels something squish up around her shoe. Looks down to see her foot sunk deep into a fresh cow-pie.

"Better watch your step. This is a pasture," says Zeke the Freak.

"Thanks for telling me," answers Joan sullenly.

They pick their way slowly up the hill. Joan is exhausted and wishes she had never come.

"Not much further," says Zeke. Joan wonders what he means by that. She knows they have come far enough to be near the next concession over from the river road. Once they get to the concession, where do they go from there? Walking along the road will be easier, but it will still be a long walk to get back to Zeke's place. Joan hears a soft low and looks behind to see a steer following behind them. As they walk the rest of the herd gradually appears over the brink of the hill. One by one, the steers fall into place alongside Joan and Zeke the Freak. Soon they are surrounded by thirty or forty animals pressing in on all sides. Joan wants to run. She starts to pick up her pace.

Zeke the Freak grabs her arm. "Slow down," he says calmly. "If you start to run, they will, too. That could be dangerous." He puts his arm around her shoulder. Every once in a while a steer presses in too close. Zeke slaps it on the side and it moves off. "They're just curious." He starts playing a game. Walks a little faster, then slower, every so often stops cold. The steers match his pace exactly. It is an eerie feeling moving among this herd of huge animals.

They get to the top of the hill. Joan had noticed a wisp of smoke pushing into the sky. No wind today so it is pluming straight up, pale white against the blue. Now she can see where it is coming from. Looking down the other side of the hill, she sees an authentic-looking teepee nestled into a corner of the field against a spur of the woods on one side and a cornfield on the other. The teepee is decorated with bright-coloured Indian symbols. Smoke is rising from the hole at the top.

"Great. Looks like somebody's there," says Zeke the Freak. As they get closer he calls out, "Hallo!"

A head pokes through the tent flap. It is Witch Doctor, the guy Joan talked to at the pig roast. His father owns the farmhouse that Zeke the Freak and Draino rent. And a whole bunch of farms around here.

"Hey, man! Zeke the Freak. Amazing!" yells Witch Doctor, stepping out of the teepee. Now Joan knows why he is called Witch Doctor.

"How's the Witch Doctor?" says Zeke the Freak.

"Running low on medicinal herbs," jokes Witch Doctor. He beams over Zeke's shoulder at Joan, pulls aside the tent flap and waves them inside.

Up close, Joan sees the teepee is made of canvas, not hides as she first thought. She is amazed at how spacious it is inside. In the centre of the floor a firepit is surrounded by neatly placed round stones. A fire is crackling brightly. Arranged around the firepit are several thick foam pads, covered with blankets and sleeping bags and strewn with pillows. It is late afternoon and the teepee, nestled close to the trees, is in full shadow. But it is warm and cosy. Witch Doctor has obviously been here awhile and the fire has had a chance to heat the place up.

"Come on in. Make yourself at home," says Witch Doctor, still smiling broadly at Joan.

Joan looks down at her muddy, wet sneakers, manure still clinging to one of them.

"I better take these off."

"Yeah, give them to me," says Zeke the Freak. "The river's just through the trees, I'll rinse 'em off and they can dry by the fire."

Joan gratefully removes her clammy socks and shoes. Zeke the Freak takes them from her and disappears through the tent flap. Joan's wet jeans slap against her ankles as she takes a seat by the fire. It is heavenly to sit at last. Steam rises from the hems of her jeans as they begin to dry off. Ranger cuddles up beside her. He looks as exhausted as she is.

"This place is fantastic."

"Isn't it great?" Witch Doctor agrees. "My sanctuary," he says with satisfaction. "I use it all year round."

"All winter?"

"Sure. The Indians did it."

Joan nods. "Yeah, I guess so." She stares into the fire.

"It's great to see you with Zeke the Freak." Joan looks up, puzzled. Witch Doctor continues, "Yeah, like I was thinking you were going out with that new guy now."

"Why do you care?" Joan asks, confused. Witch Doctor is a couple of grades below her in school and they have never hung out together. She is a town kid and he is a farmer. His family homesteaded in the area. Joan's family are still considered to be newcomers. The only time they have really talked was that time at the pig roast.

"You're good people," answers Witch Doctor, sincere warmth in his voice. "Zeke the Freak is good people, too." He leans back against a pillow, hands behind his head, wide smile still spread across his face. "You and Zeke fit in around here. The two of you being together makes sense. That new guy—I don't know about him...."

Joan smiles. For the first time since she has moved to this small town she feels accepted. She never realized before that there was anybody outside her small circle of friends who thought of her as part of the community. This guy who has roots going back for generations in the area. He says she fits in.

"I wouldn't exactly say that I'm going out with Zeke the Freak or anything...."

"Why not?" Witch Doctor suddenly gets an incensed look on his face. "Hey, man. There's nobody better. Even my dad likes him. He's been keeping our old farmhouse really great. We've never had a better renter. And he keeps the raccoons and beavers down for us, too."

"Yeah, well, I'm not so hot on this hunting stuff."

"That's because you're from town," answers Witch Doctor with a bit of a sneer. Joan feels a pang. The acceptance she felt a minute earlier is being withdrawn. "You don't see the damage raccoons do to the corn, or what beavers can do to a wood lot."

Joan is silent. Feeling abashed. It is true she has never looked at that side of it before. Zeke the Freak comes in. Sets Joan's shoes and socks on the rocks beside the fire. Looks up at Joan, then over at Witch Doctor.

"How come everybody's so down?" he asks. Without waiting for an answer, he says, "Well, I can fix that." He reaches into his pocket and pulls out a chunk of hash wrapped up in Saran Wrap. Sits down beside Joan, pats Ranger on the head. The dog is so tired he does not even open his eyes.

"Hey. Witch Doctor. Got that peace pipe of yours?"

Witch Doctor roots around and pulls out a long, carved Indian pipe with a stone bowl. "There's no pipe with a better draw," he says, holding it up proudly. "Got it on the reserve. Them Indians really know how to make a pipe."

He hands the pipe to Zeke the Freak, who unwraps the chunk of hash and starts warming it up with a match so he can break it off. It is black hash with lots of thick white lines running through it. "That's opium," says Zeke, pointing at the lines. "This is killer hash." Zeke the Freak lights up and passes the pipe to Joan. Witch Doctor takes a drag, then gets talking. All about Indians. Witch Doctor is a total maniac for Indian stuff. He talks and talks and forgets to hand on the pipe to Zeke the Freak. After a while he looks down and sees it has gone out.

"Oh, sorry, man," he apologizes.

"Don't worry," says Zeke the Freak. There is some fiddling to get the pipe lit again. Zeke takes a toke and the pipe comes back to Joan. By that time Joan is already so stoned she can hardly talk. She takes a shallow draw on the pipe and realizes she cannot handle any more. After another round the guys have had enough, too. Witch Doctor gets up and disappears into the shadows of the teepee. Comes back with a cooler and hands a beer to each of them. Just what Joan needs. She sinks into the pillows and blankets and lets herself drift. Witch Doctor continues with his monologue on Indians, Zeke the Freak interjecting from time to time. It becomes a drone to Joan's ears. She feels like her body is melting and spreading out. The darkness closes in around them until they are like a tiny planet. Three people and a dog around a fire, floating in a huge, black void.

Joan has to pee. For a long time she lies there trying to decide just how badly she has to go. Comes to the conclusion that she has to go really badly. Still takes her awhile after that to get herself to a sitting position. Flails helplessly for her shoes and socks. Zeke the Freak chuckles and helps her put them on. They are dry and toasty. Been sitting by the fire for some time. Joan peers at her watch in the firelight. It is about seven-thirty. They have been there for about three hours.

Once she gets to her feet, Joan throws herself forward, relying on momentum to get to the teepee opening. It is quite dark in the teepee, but when she has fought her way through the tent flap she sees that it is early twilight. She is still able to see well enough to make her way into the woods. Drops her jeans, crouches down, and starts to pee. And pee. And pee. And pee. Seems like the pee is never going to stop. Her thigh muscles are cramping up and she starts to feel dizzy. Afraid she is going to lose her balance and fall right on the spot where she is peeing. Finally it stops. Joan rises and has to grab onto the nearest tree until her head clears.

As she comes out of the bush she hears muffled laughter from the cornfield. "Hey, Joan, c'mere!" Zeke the Freak's voice, rustling in the field. Joan goes over to the cedar rail fence. Getting darker but she can see movement among the cornstalks about ten feet into the field. She climbs the fence and stands, trying to see where the guys are. "Get down on your knees," says Zeke. She drops down and sees the guys crouched under the cornstalks. Crawls toward them. Under the corn the light is dim. The smell of the earth rises thickly. When she gets near Zeke the Freak and Witch Doctor they scuttle off. "Tag!" screams Witch Doctor. Tag under the corn is fun. Ranger joins, too. They end up heaped together laughing helplessly. Ranger jumps on them squirming excitedly, claws gouging and tail whipping. They are too gripped with hilarity to be able to do anything about it. By then it is so dark they cannot find their way to the edge of the field. Finally Joan spots the dim glow of the teepee, lit from the inside by the fire. They make their way toward it.

Inside the teepee the fire is nearly dead. "No more wood," says Witch Doctor with regret. He stirs the embers to put it out.

"Let's go back to my place," says Zeke the Freak.

Joan is relieved to find out that it is a short walk to the road, where Witch Doctor's pickup is parked. They climb up onto the bench seat and Witch Doctor turns the ignition. The roar of the truck starting, the lights and radio coming on, bring Joan back toward reality. She is cold, dirty, and very hungry. And content. Zeke the Freak puts his arm around her shoulder and draws her close. Joan lays her head against his chest and nestles into his warmth. The truck's headlights eat up the road in front of them. A faint glimmer of sunset is caught in the rippling current of the river as they cross the bridge on their way back to Zeke's.

game boy

"Elliot is never coming back," says Joan aloud. Lying in bed, Sunday morning, staring out the window, wide awake but not quite ready to get up. Should have realized this already. Did not want to believe it before now.

Out with Zeke the Freak again last night. To the movie. Joan has been hanging around with him every weekend since Labour Day. Not really going out, just really good friends. Have not kissed yet. Not a real kiss. But they do lots of stuff and have fun together. It is nice because Sandy and Draino are really good friends, too. They all do things together. Luckily Joan has the car because it could be a real problem with only Zeke's motorcycle. Sandy and Draino are more than just good friends. Lots of times when they are out driving, Joan looks in her rear-view mirror and Sandy and Draino have disappeared into the darkness of the back seat.

"I guess I am going out with Zeke." Again aloud to herself. Surprised. Never thought she would be saying anything like that. Can now see that Zeke was the right guy for her all along. They could have had a gas together all summer. Sandy, Draino, she and Zeke. If she had seen this sooner. All that time and trouble spent avoiding Zeke. What a waste.

Watches a squirrel ply the branches of the big maple tree outside her window. Joan's muscles are twitching to get moving. But she does not want to leave her warm bed. Furnace does not get turned on until they have to wear parkas around the house. Her father never wants to admit that winter is coming. It is Thanksgiving weekend. That should be soon enough, thinks Joan. But her parents have gone away until Sunday and they left it off. Not sure what has to be done to get it started.

Joan smiles. She has the house to herself. They trusted her enough to let her stay home alone. For the first time. Went to stay with friends in Barrie. For both nights of the long weekend. No objections at all when Joan said she had shifts at the steak house Saturday and Sunday. Joan gets a surge of energy. Throws off the covers, scoops up her clothes and sprints downstairs to the kitchen. Oil space heater in the kitchen. The one room in the house that is warm during the fall months before her father decides it is time to get the furnace going.

Joan dresses in the kitchen. Puts the kettle on. Sits and looks around the large kitchen with satisfaction. Can eat breakfast in peace. No mother reading and tsking at the articles in the local paper. Father not there to comment on how late she got in last night. And she got in very late. She, Zeke, Sandy, and Draino went to the late movie because she had to work the dinner shift. Then to the drive-in, then drove around for a long time. Warm twinge thinking about Zeke. Zeke the Freak. How could she have not seen it earlier? She and Zeke are good together.

Today it is the lunch and afternoon shift. Working the coffee shop. Pretty quiet. Most people are doing family dinners. The odd fisherman comes in. Up from the harbour to get warm. Mostly they stay down at the water in truck trailers they drive up from the city. The tail end of the tourist season. Sportsmen, they call themselves. As far as Joan can see they spend most of their time drinking beer in their trailers. There are three of them sitting in the corner booth right now. All probably in their forties, beer bellies, nicotine-stained fingers. Wearing plaid shirts over T-shirts that do not quite meet the tops of their pants. They have been there for about an hour and have had their coffees refilled a number of times. Free refills, that is Steve's policy. Joan thinks it is overly generous in a situation like this. She has had to run back and forth to their table one too many times now. Especially because they keep asking her on dates. Sort of jokingly, but she thinks they would jump on it if she agreed.

Joan sits at the lunch counter. On the stool that is the farthest away from their table. Trying not to make eye contact. That means staring straight ahead of her at the glass-fronted cooler where the pies are lined up on shelves. Nobody ever orders pies. There is banana cream, and coconut cream, and something pink-coloured. Odd time when somebody does order a slice a kind of nervous look passes over Steve's face. Pies in the cooler today have probably been there for about a month. Joan is thinking of offering the fishermen slices on the house. Decides that would probably encourage them. Props her chin up with her hands and stares past the pies to her reflection in the mirrored back of the cooler.

Deep in a daydream. The sound of the bells on the door makes her jump. Prince Charming comes in. Smiles when he sees her. Very casually, but deliberately comes over and sits down beside her. Joan freezes. Thinks it would be rude to get up and move away. Does not really want to sit with Prince Charming, either. Glances over her shoulder and sees the fishermen are getting their jackets on. With relief she jumps up and waits at the cash register for them to pay. Looks back at Prince Charming and holds her finger up to signal that she will be with him in a minute.

The fishermen leave. As the door closes behind them she hears a muttered comment about a "faggy boyfriend". They really were hanging around with high hopes, she realizes. At least when Prince Charming came in it cleared them out. Joan goes back to him but stays behind the counter instead of taking her stool again.

"Do you want a menu?" she asks.

146 — *Mary Jo Pallak*

"No, thanks, just a coffee."

She pours him one, then goes over to the fishermen's table to
clear it off. It is a mess with sugar spilled everywhere, damp nap-
kins covering coffee spills, ripped-apart creamers, and cigarette
butts ground into saucers. Takes her awhile to get it cleaned up.
Tucked under one of the cups is a dime—that is the only tip.
"Jerk-offs," she says under her breath. Feels Prince Charming's
eyes following her. Her cheeks start to burn. Finally she cannot
avoid looking up at him. He smiles at her again.

"Have a coffee with me."

"God. I've had four or five already this aft."

Prince Charming sort of leans forward and looks up at her.
His hair hangs in a fringy swatch over his eyes, but she can still
see the extra-blueness of them underneath. Looking very serious.
Joan breathes in deeply, the heat in her cheeks spreading to her
neck. He is really absolutely the most foxiest guy she has ever
met. He does not say anything but breaks the gaze. Pulls a pack-
age of cigarettes out of his jacket pocket and sticks one in his
mouth. Offers the pack to her. She shrugs and takes one. He
lights hers first, then his.

"You get all weird around me," he says without looking up.

"Do I?" In a put-on, innocent voice that sounds fake, even to
her.

"Yeah. Like right now, for instance."

Joan's eyes fix on a spot on the floor. A chipped tile. She
keeps staring at it while she blurts out, "It's this father-son
thing...." She surprises herself with her own bluntness, but he
does not seem to be taken aback.

"I thought that's what it might be..."

She interrupts. "I saw you and him leaving the chicken barbeque with that girl. She looked pretty young. And how come
you're only interested in out-of-town girls."

"You're right. She was too young. My dad got carried away."
Joan's mouth falls open. She looks up at Prince Charming.
Almost afraid of what she is going to hear next. Prince
Charming sees the expression on her face. "It's not what you

think, though. My dad does photography. For a while he's been doing this series...um...mostly of me with girls." He pauses. "It's all really artistic, though. There's really nothing sexy about the pictures. We thought it was really best not to use local girls. It's to protect the girls as well as us."

"What do you mean?"

"Well...um...the pictures are nude."

"Oh," says Joan.

"Here—let me show you." He reaches inside his jacket and brings out a sheaf of black and white, eight by ten photographs. Lays them on the counter. Joan looks down and sees a beautiful image of Prince Charming and a girl lying back-to-back. Both staring at the camera, faces blank. Arms crossed in x's over their chests, with hands on their shoulders. Backs pressed together, knees bent, soles of each other's feet touching. Prince Charming is right, it is not at all erotic. A composition of light and shadow, symmetry of form. Joan also sees that Prince Charming's body is completely amazing. She fans the photos out. They all have a soulful innocent quality. Although they are nude, the poses are all pretty modest.

"These are really good," she murmurs.

"I think so." Prince Charming takes a gulp of his coffee and a drag on his cigarette. "Dad is still really interested in using you."

"I don't think I could do that," she answers.

"We would never show them around here."

"Even still."

"We wouldn't expect you to just strip down right away. We'd start with shots of us in underwear or swimsuits. We wouldn't expect you to go any further than you are comfortable."

It still gives Joan the creeps. "No, really," she says.

"Well, think about it. I know you're interested in art. Don't limit yourself to small-town thinking."

Joan bristles. "What makes you think it has anything to do with small-town thinking?"

"Okay, whatever you say."

Joan frowns. There is no way she is going to pose. Even if

Prince Charming thinks that makes her a small-town girl.

"Maybe you'd like to see a movie with me tonight."

Joan looks up to see the piercing blue eyes, very sincere behind the blond bangs.

"Oh. Thanks. But I've got plans already."

"Yeah. Pretty short notice. Sorry. How about next weekend?"

Prince Charming is asking her out! She will be the envy of every girl at school. Starts thinking about how she will let it drop. No. Lots of people will see her at the movie with him. Can she wait until next weekend for everybody to find out? Joan stops herself. Maybe he is only asking her out to loosen her up so that she will pose for his father.

Like he has read her mind he says, "I don't care if you pose or not. I think you're the only girl at the high school who's interesting."

She swells with pride. Looks at Prince Charming to see if he is serious. Seems like he is. Then she remembers what she told herself this morning. She is going out with Zeke the Freak.

"I'm kinda seeing somebody already," she answers him.

"That guy with the motorcycle? He looks pretty cool."

"Yeah, he is," she says with a smile. He really is, she thinks.

The bell on the door tinkles. Sandy comes in. Walks to the end of the counter where Joan and Prince Charming are. A bubble of cold air still clings to her. Joan shivers.

Sandy looks up at the clock. "I thought maybe Steve might let you go early."

Joan looks up. Still half an hour before her shift is up. If Prince Charming were not here she could call Steve out and show him the empty coffee shop. Looks at Prince Charming and feels a slight pang. He really is a hunk. Again it's like he reads her mind. Prince Charming rises from the stool, zips up his jacket.

"Nice talking to you," he says to Joan, with a smile that makes her insides wobble. Gives Sandy a nod and heads out the door. Joan clears away his cup and saucer and wipes up the counter. Realizes with a start that he has not paid. Shrugs to herself. All he had was a coffee. Steve pokes his head out the kitchen door, sees the place is deserted. Joan does not have to ask. He makes a shooing motion with his hands, letting her know she is free to leave.

"What were you talking about with Prince Charming?" asks Sandy. In the car on their way to the Farmhouse. Tonight Zeke the Freak and Draino are preparing a Thanksgiving Feast for them.

"Oh, nothing," says Joan, hoping to evade the issue.

"I think he likes you," teases Sandy.

"Well, he did ask me out." Joan cannot keep a slight boasting tone from her voice.

Sandy squeals. "When?"

"He asked me to the movies next Saturday, but I'm not going."

"What?"

"I'm going out with Zeke the Freak," answers Joan with a little irritation.

"I don't remember any wedding," shoots Sandy sarcastically.

Joan is silent. Glares at the road ahead of her. After a while she says in a flat voice, "I believe in making commitments."

They reach the driveway to the Farmhouse and turn in. The house is glowing warmly in the late afternoon sun, windowpanes flaring with brightness. The oranges and reds of the trees surrounding the place are accentuated against a deep, blue sky. A calendar picture. In her mind Joan can see "Brown's Co-op—All Your Feed and Fertilizer Needs" written underneath it. As they pull up to the house, Draino's face appears in the kitchen window. He waves, then disappears. Joan and Sandy get out of the car and go in without knocking. Before they can get their jackets off, Ranger is wiggling his body around their legs. Joan is almost knocked over before she can get him calmed down.

Zeke the Freak is working over the stove. The air in the kitchen is dense with warm cooking smells. Aside from the immediate mess of Zeke's food preparation, the room is spotlessly tidy. Low rays of the sun make a dazzling path across the freshly shined floor. Table already set for six people. Draino is sitting at the table, talking to Witch Doctor, who is with a girl. They are sitting close together on the kitchen couch. Joan has not seen Witch Doctor's girlfriend before. Wonders where she is from.

"It's the girls!" calls Witch Doctor to Joan and Sandy as they pull off their jackets. "I'd like you to meet my lady, Jewel."

"What's your lady-jewel's name?" asks Sandy without guile.

"That's her name," Witch Doctor answers. Annoyed. "Jewel."

"Oh…neat," says Sandy.

"Hi," says Joan, smiling at Jewel. She and Sandy sit down at the table with Draino. They all smoke a joint. Zeke drifts over from the stove for a couple of tokes. Does not sit down. Working intensely on the creation of the feast. Their Thanksgiving dinner. Joan gets up and goes to his side.

"Want a hand?"

"I'm okay. Got the whole thing all timed out. Shouldn't be much longer."

Joan is glad to hear that. Munchies have set in. Smells in the kitchen are driving her wild with hunger. Looks at meat in a roasting pan that Zeke has just pulled out of the oven. "What is that?" she asks, staring at the unfamiliar shape resting in a bed of potatoes, onions, and carrots.

"Beaver," answers Zeke in a matter-of-fact tone. Pulls out another pan. "This one here is raccoon. I don't know what it's going to be like, but I thought I'd give it a try." He looks up at her and grins. "Got all these carcasses in the freezer from hunting and trapping. Seems a shame to let 'em go to waste." Takes the lid off a pot on the stove to show her what looks like six tiny chickens. "These here are squab. Shot 'em out of the rafters in the barn."

"Squab?" says Sandy.

"Just a fancy name for pigeons," says Zeke. By this time he is laying the feast out on serving dishes and setting them on the table. Besides the three meat dishes, he has made wild rice with nuts and beans and a big bowl of squash. Joan is not the only one with the munchies. Silence around the table as they eat. Except for appreciative moans and sighs. At the end, groans of overindulgence.

"The raccoon I can take or leave, but the beaver and squab were scrump-dilly-icious," pronounces Witch Doctor.

"Everything was really good," agrees Jewel. "Excuse me, I have to go to the bathroom," she says shyly and leaves the table. Witch Doctor watches her leave. Adoring expression on his face.

"Where's Jewel from?" asks Joan.

"Over by Blythe," answers Witch Doctor. "That's where you want to get a girl." Witch Doctor's eyes kind of wink and twinkle. He is looking at Zeke and Draino. "You're wasting your time with these beach-town girls. Always acting so sophisticated, always looking for rich tourist guys." Joan and Sandy pretend to get incensed. "Seriously," Witch Doctor goes on, "get yourself an inland girl. They fuck like minks. Got nothing else to do. And they're dying to get out of town or off the farm, so they're grateful to most any guy who will pay them attention."

It makes Joan uncomfortable that Witch Doctor is talking this way. She looks up and sees Jewel is in the doorway. She has heard most of what Witch Doctor has said. Does not seem to mind. Giggles a bit. Joan is taken aback. She has always thought of farm girls as being "virgin-until-marriage" types. Then she thinks of Helena, a big, buxom farm girl in her class at high school. Sits with a group in a corner of the cafeteria at lunchtime, reading the Bible. Then goes out to the parking lot with her boyfriend to neck in his car. Just about everybody in the school claims to have caught them fucking, although Joan has never seen them doing anything except heavy petting when she has happened to pass by.

"What's for dessert?" asks Witch Doctor.

Zeke does not say anything for a minute. Finally he quietly utters, "Uh-oh."

"No dessert?" Several voices chime in.

"I don't want any dessert. I'm stuffed," states Joan.

"Got to have pumpkin pie on Thanksgiving!" asserts Witch Doctor. Draino, Sandy, and Jewel nod their heads in agreement.

"We could go get some," says Draino.

"Yeah, let's go get some! I bet the Highway Market is open."

Sandy looks at Joan. "Give us a ride to the Highway Market."

"I don't even like pumpkin pie," complains Joan.

"We can go in my truck," offers Witch Doctor.

Seems like it takes only a second for Witch Doctor, Jewel, Sandy, and Draino to clear out of the kitchen. Sudden silence leaves Joan feeling stunned. Sits and stares at the vestiges of the feast. After a while she picks up a couple of dishes and starts to carry them toward the sink.

"Uh, uh, uh!" Zeke waves a finger in the air. "Put those down. The dishes can wait. Look what I have here." Zeke opens a cupboard and brings out a bottle. "Recognize this?"

Joan squints at the label. After a minute she realizes what it is. She grins. "Richie Rich's sherry," she says, chuckling.

Zeke laughs. "Still don't have any sherry glasses." He gets a tumbler out of the cupboard and fills it for her. Hands it to her and starts rolling a doob. Joan stares at the glass. Not sure exactly what sherry is. Something her grandmother used to drink. Joan thinks it might be like wine. She has had a few beers and she knows you are not supposed to mix wine and beer. Decides that if her grandmother drank it, it must not be very strong. They sit down on the couch side by side and toke a good part of the joint. After that Joan lights up a cigarette and swigs the sherry.

"I'm not much of a dessert man myself. Didn't even think of it. Sorry."

"'S'okay," Joan slurs. Her tongue is not moving very easily in her mouth. "Ga go t'th bathr'm." Lurches herself off the couch and reels toward the stairs. Stairs look too steep. Thinks she will pee her pants, though, so she forces herself to make the climb. Feels delicious to sit on the toilet and let the pee spill out. Also to have her jeans undone because her stomach is bloated from overeating. Thinking of the feast makes her feel sick. She barely has time to get to her knees on the floor to puke into the toilet. The smell of the pee in the toilet makes her even sicker and she keeps retching long after she has thrown up everything there is to throw up. Joan gets the toilet flushed and drags herself up to the sink. Rinses out her mouth and wipes off her face. Checks to see if there are any puke bits on her clothing.

Opens the bathroom door to go downstairs. Realizes she is not going to make it. Thinks about lying down on the floor in the hallway. She is leaning against the door jamb. Looks up and sees Zeke's bedroom. From where she is the bed is only a few feet away. Joan launches herself forward and throws herself onto the bed. Cannot move. Lies face-down in the dark and quiet. Smell of Zeke on the bed cover. Sound of music drifts up the stairs. Zeke has put a record on the turntable. Joan hears dishes clattering. Then she passes out.

Wakes up to being rolled over by Zeke. With little effort he slips her jeans off. How did he do that? she thinks. Her jeans are pretty tight. Joan cannot get them off that fast herself. Next he is unbuttoning her shirt. Makes no move to stop him. Mainly because she cannot seem to move her muscles. Lies limply. Zeke covers her with his body. His full weight feels good and soft and warm. His nose and lips press into the hollow under her ear. Kisses her repeatedly from one side of the neck to the other. His lips move up to her mouth. She can taste that he has just brushed his teeth. Wonders how her mouth tastes. Must be very gross-tasting, especially with his nice clean mouth.

Next thing she knows, both her shirt and her bra are off. The air in the bedroom is a bit chilly and her groggy fog is lifting. Still cannot move. Zeke is cupping her breasts, one in each hand. Nuzzling his face between them, sucking her nipples. A sweet aching has begun to pulse between her legs. The fuzziness in her head is replaced by a swimming dizziness.

Now her panties have been removed. Joan thinks Zeke must practice some kind of clothes-removing magic, it has all happened so fast. His clothes, too, have disappeared. For the first time in her life Joan can see what an erect cock looks like. Sort of threatening. Zeke the Freak is straddling her on his knees. Looming above her on the the bed. He lowers his face to hers and presses his tongue between her lips. At the same time he brings his hips down and the tip of his cock comes in contact with the throbbing part of her. A tingling feeling radiates in waves from this focal point. Pleasure washing over her body like she has never felt before. The throbbing rushes to her face, pounding at her cheeks from the inside.

Zeke's cock is probing between her legs. Beginning to make headway, parting flesh, pushing up inside her. A furrow plows across Joan's forehead.

"Wait."

Joan brings her hands up to Zeke's shoulders and tries to fend him off. He is suddenly like a snarling animal. Grabs her wrists and pins her arms into the pillows on either side of her. Overpowering strength. Joan cannot struggle free—his grip is like iron and his weight on her body like lead.

"Oh, no, you don't," he grunts, "I've waited too long for this."

"We have to talk...."

"Don't be a fuckin' tease! You can't just stop a guy right in the middle." A forceful stab. His cock rips up into her.

Joan inhales sharply and screams, "Ouch! Jesus Fuck! That hurts. Stop."

Zeke does not stop. Several more thrusts. Joan feels his sperm squirting inside her. He goes limp on top of her. She feels his cock soften up and slip out. Sticky wetness leaks between her thighs and pools on the sheet under her bum. Zeke is a dead weight pressing down on her. Joan gasps for breath. He mumbles, "Oh, sorry," and rolls over to lie beside her. Joan lies on her back, staring at the ceiling. She is shocked and numb. Very confused. Angry that Zeke the Freak did not stop when she wanted to.

"Thank god I am on the pill," she whispers to herself. The pill she started taking because she thought she would lose her virginity to Elliot.

Joan turns her head to look at Zeke. Snoozing with a satisfied grin on his face. She remembers the commitment she made in her mind to Zeke today. Runs the palm of her hand over the curve of his chest. The sweet aching feeling wells up in her again. Shivers crawl up her spine at the thought of his cock between her legs. Moves closer to Zeke and lays her head on his chest. His smile spreads wider and he throws an arm over her.

Joan has been dozing. Wakes to the sound of a car coming up the driveway. Does not know if a minute has passed by, or an hour. Sandy, Draino, and the others back from town, she thinks. With dessert. She realizes she is very hungry. Car door slams. Ranger is at the foot of the bed. He perks up his head and barks tentatively. Zeke the Freak gives him a bit of a kick and he quiets down. Kitchen door closes. They are in the house now, she thinks. Joan waits for Sandy's voice calling her. All she can hear is somebody walking around downstairs. Pausing now and then, as if looking for something. Joan hears footsteps coming up the stairs. Bedroom door flies open. She cannot make out who it is against the light spilling in from the hallway.

"Elliot!" yelps Zeke. He leaps to his feet and bounces across the bed to the doorway. Joan snatches at the covers which Zeke has thrown off, pulling them up around her chin. Ranger starts jumping all over the bed and barking. Joan has to cover her face to keep from being whipped by his tail. "Great to see you, man," yells Zeke over the barking. Gives Elliot a big hug. Elliots acts like he is annoyed and mumbles something about fags. Zeke laughs and backs off. Grabs his jeans off the bed and pulls them on.

"Hi, Joan," says Elliot over Zeke's shoulder, with a teasing tone in his voice. He gives her a little wave and turns around to go back downstairs. Zeke follows close on Elliot's heels, Ranger close on Zeke's.

Joan sits on the bed, bundled in the blanket. Could not see Elliot very well. He did not say very much. Did he seem glad to see her? Disappointed to find her in bed with Zeke the Freak?

Joan sighs. It does not matter anyhow. There has to be some point where a person decides on something and then does not go back. All the same. It would have been nice to have had the chance to make a choice. If she could have held Zeke off a little longer. If he had paid attention to her and stopped when she wanted him to. If Zeke had not raped her....

Anxiety tightens her chest. "Oh, my God." Her voice wavering, she pulls the blankets closer around her and begins to sob. Should have stopped him sooner. She takes several deep breaths to try and calm down. "No!" she says out loud. Zeke is a good guy. Good people, like Witch Doctor says. Already decided this morning to start a serious relationship with him. He really cares for her. Just got carried away.

Joan bursts into tears again. Zeke is beside her, crushing her against him. "Hey, baby, it's all right," he coos. "No, no, no. Don't cry. Everything is beautiful."

"Why didn't you stop? I wasn't ready!"

"Oh, man," he groans, "you know you wanted it."

"I wasn't ready. I asked you to stop. You just kept on going...you forced me..." She is shuddering with tears. Cannot even think how to say what is in her head. Kind of stutters, "...it was like...you raped me."

"That's a load of shit," he sneers. "You were primed and ready. You can't rape a woman that's primed and ready. You came even before I got inside you."

Joan remembers the intense pleasure that washed over her. At first. Before his cock got inside her. Was that an orgasm? Must have been. If she had an orgasm then it could not have been rape. Could it?

Zeke the Freak gives her another crushing hug. "Hey, Joan. C'mon downstairs. Elliot has something that'll cheer you up."

Joan gets her clothes on and goes downstairs. Finds Zeke and Elliot sitting at the kitchen table. No sign of the feast. Must have been passed out for quite a while before Zeke came upstairs. Would have taken him some time to clean up and put everything away. Joan sits down at the table beside Zeke. There are several rows of white powder arranged on a record-album cover in front of Elliot.

"What's that?" she asks.

"I brought it back from Calgary. Everybody is doing it out there…. Cocaine."

"Yeah," says Zeke enthusiastically. "I've been wanting to try it for a long time. I heard it's the perfect drug. Doesn't fuck up your body. Actually clears your head! Just makes you feel wonderful. And you don't get addicted. It's natural, too. The Incas in Peru have been doing it for thousands of years."

Joan has heard of the Incas chewing coca leaves. She has also heard all sorts of stories about it being in Coca-Cola when it was first invented and people getting addicted. She has read that it was the coolest drug and all sorts of stars used it. Rock stars and movie stars. In places like Regine's and Studio 54. Places she has read about in magazines. Places she has dreamed about going to. She has never heard of anybody around here doing it yet. She thinks this is probably the first time somebody brought any to town.

"Can I try some?" she asks.

"You're with me, babe," says Zeke, pulling her close to him, "so you're in." He looks into her eyes and smiles. She smiles at him. Elliot smiles, too.